Dark Tea

by

Ash Warren

A Penelope Middleton Mystery

For Linda and Geoffrey

Chapter 1

Prepare for Rain.

April 28th, 1591.
Jurakudai, Kyoto.

Most Venerable Abbot,

Forgive me for not writing to you sooner and sharing with you the most recent news concerning the Master, which is something I know you have perhaps been waiting anxiously to hear. Had I been able, I would have sent this letter to you some days ago, but to tell the truth, these are dark days.

In our deep despair, many of us who were there on his last night have been unable to eat or sleep since that time, nor have any of us felt safe. As a result, most of us have now fled the capital and scattered to the four winds lest we face the wrath of the *kampaku*, who increasingly tends to see enemies everywhere, even when there are none. I have also had to heed my better judgment and leave this place lest action is taken against me.

The Master, as you know, was sentenced to commit suicide some days ago now, and I can report that he carried out this final act of obedience on the twenty-first day of the fourth month at the hour of the Ox. It gives me no small pride to be able to tell you that he faced his end with both courage and the serenity that befits a master of our Way of Tea, and at no time showed the slightest weakness or fear, even at the final moment.

Despite our best efforts, none of us, Most Venerable One, have been able to understand why our Master was so suddenly sentenced to death, and I am sad to say that this includes myself.

Many rumors abound. Some say it was because some of his enemies, who were envious of his power and position as a trusted advisor to the *kampaku*, and poured poison into our Lord's ears and that this inspired him to lash out in anger at our Master. Others said it was because of some pettiness involving a statue he had made of himself and displayed in a way that gave the *kampaku* offense, and still others maintained it was because he spoke out against our Lord's intended campaign in Korea.

It seems unlikely we will ever know the truth, as the *kampaku* himself has shown an unwillingness to discuss the matter further, as is often the way of mighty lords such as he. All that really matters though, is that his will was carried out and that our Master acquitted himself with honor in the doing of it. For this, all of us are grateful, and, though wracked with sadness at his passing, we stand together more in awe of him now than even when he walked among us. As you have said, true greatness often shows itself in how we face our deaths, and this was doubly true of our Master.

It only falls to me now, Most Venerable One, to describe to you his final hours and how they were spent, and not to dwell overmuch on the moment of his death. To have been with him then was to see how a true Tea Master should meet his end, celebrating until the very last moment the beauties of our art to which he dedicated his whole life.

Let me tell you briefly how his last evening transpired.

I must say, first of all, how gracious it was of the *kampaku* Hideyoshi to extend to our Master these last few days, and for him thus to be able to prepare not only for his own end but also for the gathering we were able to attend. On hearing of his sentence, many of us had left our homes and rushed to the capital to be with him, and indeed the whole city has spoken of little else since the sentence was handed down.

On that final night of his life, the Master invited his closest friends and disciples, a group of men we both have the honor to be counted among, for a last tea gathering at the Jurakudai villa, where he remained at the request of the *kampaku* in order to carry out the final sentence.

On that final evening, Most Venerable One, about twenty of us gathered as instructed at the Jurakudai to attend a final tea ceremony, which, as you can imagine, was an evening none of us will ever forget. The Jurakudai is a very great estate, as befits a mighty lord such as the *kampaku*, and the rooms wherein the master resided were spacious and well appointed.

The final gathering was held in one of these rooms. Therein we saw the most beautiful tea equipment, including a wonderful scroll and the flower display the Master had arranged with his own hand. I have the pleasure to inform you it was a simple wreath of cherry blossom, as befitted not only the season but also the idea of the transience of life itself. The scroll he chose to display was also powerful in its message, and bore the single character 'life,' which made several of us break into tears the moment we laid eyes on it.

I cannot help but think, Most Venerable One, that in some ways, these two things were a kind of rebuke to the *kampaku*, a way of saying that even as his final command was to be carried out, that in effect, he had no power over our Master, nor of any of us. All of us will pass away, like the falling blossom, and none of us are compelled by any man to this existence or the next.

We were all served a final meal, as is common in our Way of Tea, of seasonable vegetables, which were beautifully and simply arranged, and also a bowl of fragrant rice and sake. This meal was eaten in silence, but the Master moved among us, served us the sake, and bade us talk a little with him. I must admit that when my turn came, my hand trembled as I held out my cup for him to fill, and tears coursed down my face. But the master smiled and told me not to fear for him, and that all was exactly as it should be.

After our meal, he made tea for us, giving us one last chance to see his consummate skill. His concentration, and also his solitude, were apparent for all to see, and we all knew that once again, we were in the presence of the very greatest master of our age. His tea was gracious and powerful, just as he was, and as I raised the bowl to my lips, I was overcome with the sheer beauty of our Way, and once again, my tears wet the sleeves of my robes.

At the end, Most Venerable One, our Master presented us each with a gift. Some of us received bowls and other equipment that he had made, others precious scrolls by great priests and calligraphers, and some just simple things like a tea scoop or a whisk, or even a letter. All was done with perfect taste and a feeling of brotherhood and deep affection.

When we could delay no longer, our Master told us to take our leave and to continue to perfect our practice.

And this was the last I ever saw of him.

One of us, our brother the Lord Oribe, remained behind to assist our Master with his final passage.

According to him, a white cloth was spread upon the floor, and our Master, dressed in white robes, mounted a small dais that had been placed in the center.

He took the bowl with which he had made tea for us and broke it, as a sign that none should ever drink the tea of sadness again.

Then he wrote his final poem, which Lord Oribe now has in his possession.

A life of seventy years,
Strength spent to the very last
With this my jewelled sword,
I kill both patriarchs and buddhas.
I yet carry one article I had gained
The long sword
And now at this moment
I hurl it to the heavens.

Our master, kneeling, pulled open his robes and cut open his stomach.

He showed no fear, and greeted his death with complete equanimity.

Most Venerable One, there is nothing more to tell.

I hope to see you soon, and to answer any questions you might have, but for the present moment, let us remember him, our great master, Sen no Rikyu, the founder of our Way of Tea.

Your servant

Ujisato Gamo

Chapter 2

An Old Box

It would have taken almost no time to destroy the fragile old building, a straightforward job with the backhoe they had brought with them. Still, all the same, it was something that brought a moment of sadness to Yusuke Okamoto, who headed up the small Kamakura-based construction company that had been tasked with knocking it down and clearing the ground for the new building that was planned.

Yusuke came from an old Kamakura family and knew that the old town of Kamakura was more than a little resistant to change, like many old Japanese towns. Many would just prefer to shutter their shops and lose their railways, post offices, and schools than embark on any major change that violated the old residents' way of life.

It was just the way they were.

However, Kamakura was a little different from these old places far away from the big cities. While many similar towns in Japan were in danger of disappearing due to the aging society, the low birth rate, and the constant migration of young people to the cities, Kamakura, with its many charms, was still hanging on in being able to maintain its old ways.

And that was what people who lived there, and those who visited from nearby Tokyo, liked about the place.

It held its history close, and its ghosts still walked its streets in the misty rainy season and the quiet snow of its winters. It had plenty of history to share as well, even though there was little vestige of the power it had once had when the first *shogun* had chosen it to be the capital some eight centuries prior. Memories, however, lingered in other ways.

The early *shoguns* favored the new religion of Zen Buddhism, and as a result, the old town was filled with some of the oldest and most important temples in the country, serene and dignified places where time seemed to stand still. It also hosted some important pageants and other historical performances every year, and of course, it was home to the Great Buddha of Kamakura, which was an important tourist draw, and also many of the temples, such as the famous Meigetsu-in, had lavish and wonderful gardens that drew people from across the country and earned the town's nickname of 'little Kyoto.'

In short, Kamakura had a reputation for sedate and old-fashioned charm, a quiet place to escape the bustle of the capital, and a place where neighbors, who had known each other's families for generations, still took pride in their old family homes and businesses. And because Kamakura was still regarded as such a beautiful place to live, the town had long been the home to many of Japan's most well-known artists and writers, a tradition that continues to this day. This, of course, did a fair bit for the local real estate industry in the elevation of prices to a level that few could afford; however, there were still places to be had where it was possible to find an old home in the hills or near the shore which had charms that were often totally lacking in the capital.

Places like Kamakura had tradition in their blood and bones, and regarded change, when it came, as something to be resisted if at all possible.

The Okamoto family had started their family business hundreds of years before as carpenters working on the big temples and shrines in the area, places that were constantly in need of restoration or other work. Today though, most of their work was in building new houses in the nearby Shonan area, where there were several new developments, or working on apartment complexes as well as occasionally clearing away old homes when the owners died so that they could be replaced with new ones. Business wasn't that great, and the economy had not been good for years, but there was still a steady trickle of work for an old family like theirs, so the brothers managed to make a decent living.

However, it wasn't often that you were called in to destroy an old building like the one today, and this one was very old indeed.

For one thing, it still had the traditional thatched roof, which you rarely saw even in places like Kamakura these days, and old white mud and plaster walls that were never used anymore except in historical buildings. The family, however, had done plenty of work in helping to restore Kamakura's many ancient temples, so they were very familiar with this type of thing.

Yusuke guessed the tea house, for that was the purpose of the old building, must be at least two hundred years old, and it made him a little sad to be getting rid of a piece of his hometown's history rather than seeing it restored.

Nevertheless, the owners were right. Even a quick look with an experienced eye like his revealed that all the wooden beams were rotten to the foundations, and the roof not only leaked but could have caved in at any time, which was the reason that the tea house wasn't used, and hadn't been for almost twenty years.

Sadly, it was definitely a hazard, and now the time had come for it to go.

Being a tea house, there was not a lot inside it. The first job had been to take out all the rotten old tatami mats, which he and his brother Ichiro had dragged outside and thrown in the big dumpster they had brought with them. After that, they began to knock down the inside walls with their sledgehammers. It was not a pleasant job, and they were both soon wearing masks and protective glasses, as every time they struck the old plaster walls, a cloud of dust would rise up in their faces, so much so that they could barely breathe.

Yusuke had just gone outside for some fresh air and a moment of relief from the dust when he heard his brother calling him from inside.

"What?" he shouted through the little doorway. All tea houses had this funny little entrance you had to crawl through, which was something about everyone being equal or some such thing.

"Found something in the wall. An old box. You want to see it?"

"Sure," said Yusuke and crawled back into the dusty old room, which was now just bare boards and rubble with half the inner walls missing.

Ichiro was carefully extracting an old, rusted metal box from the wall, which he placed on the floor between them.

"Whoa... that looks interesting..." he said, bending down to examine it. "We better tell old Takahashi, I guess. Might be something that belongs to his family."

He had seen quite a few old boxes and cases like this before in old houses and had dug up quite a number from underneath them. He had even found a few that were stuffed with money that no one had known existed, which was a pretty common find for construction crews in Japan. Many old people liked to keep their cash 'under the tatami,' as it was known, as they didn't trust banks, something the Okamoto family found completely understandable. Not trusting the banks or the government to do anything for you was a trait the Japanese shared with their far-away neighbors, the French, and with almost the same enthusiasm.

The old box was black with age and had the kind of ornate metal clasps you found on boxes from hundreds of years ago in the Edo Period. The whole thing was almost rusted through, and it would be a simple job to open it with the end of a hammer if you had to. But the Okamoto family were honest folk and would not dream of damaging anything that belonged to someone else.

Together they carefully brought the old box up to the main house, where the maid asked them to wait while she got the master.

===================

The Takahashi School of the Japanese Tea Ceremony was one of the most venerable and significant of the Japanese tea ceremony schools in the Kanto region, including the capital city of Tokyo and the regions around it. It dated back to the mid-seventeenth century and had always been based in Kamakura, where generations of tea masters had studied and from whence it had gained a national fame. The school now boasted a large compound with several small teahouses in its extensive gardens, and an elegant Meiji period mansion which was still the Takahashi family home.

The head of the school, who bore the hereditary title of *iemoto*, or Grandmaster, was the 14th Grandmaster Tomohisa Takahashi, a man of few friends, great impatience, and an occasionally vile temper, who lived with his two grown-up children, Issei and Momoko, and his second wife Haruko, a good-looking young woman who was not that much older than his daughter. He was not a man much given for socializing unless he had to, found most people extremely bothersome, and had little time for his family. Yet, apart from the tea ceremony, he did have time for money, and that was his overriding concern these days.

Although the older and far bigger Urasenke and Omotesenke tea schools based in Kyoto were still prosperous, the whole of the Japanese tea ceremony world had been in a steady state of decline for the last fifty years, and none more so than the smaller schools such as his own. With this near continuous decline in income that had come with fewer and fewer students had also come a disastrous lessening in status for people like himself, who had now become the type of folk that belonged to a previous time and were more and more regarded as an anachronism, rather than as an integral part of Japanese high society.

Gone were the days of invitations to the Palace to conduct the tea ceremony for the Imperial Family or to act as tutors to the young princesses. Gone also were the Japanese aristocracy who used to patronize them and the honors that were occasionally bestowed by the government for their tireless work in preserving Japanese culture on behalf of a grateful nation.

The main reason for this was very simple: women. Or rather the changes that had taken place for Japanese women since the end of the War.

Learning the tea ceremony had once been de rigueur and an essential part of a good education for any well-bred Japanese girl. It was where they learned good manners, how to dress properly, how to behave in society, and especially how to serve and act when with one's husband and his friends in the correct manner. Learning the tea ceremony was a university degree in correct etiquette at a time when very few women ever darkened the doors of an institution like a finishing school and where today increasingly few families had any idea what it constituted. Almost no family in the old days failed to ensure that their daughters were able to perform the tea ceremony, and even now it was still a basic form of training for *geisha* and others involved in the classical arts.

But those days, needless to say, were now kaput.

Although 95% of people enrolled in the tea schools were still women, the numbers had dropped precipitously in the last several decades, and none more so than in the present one. To be fair, this decline was not only limited to the tea ceremony but all the classical Japanese arts, including Japanese dance, calligraphy, flower arrangement, musical instruments such as the *koto* and *shamisen*, and so on. Most women these days thought of these things as something their grandmothers (or even great-grandmothers) did, and wore *kimono*, the mode of dress commonly worn at tea ceremonies, maybe once or twice in their lives - those being their college graduations or at their weddings.

The times were moving, and even such august traditions as the tea ceremony had to move with them or perish. It seemed, though, that the latter was by far the more likely outcome.

Such were the things weighing on the mind of the *iemoto* this morning as he sat in his well-appointed sitting room having his morning cup of coffee and reading the newspaper.

He usually rose late, but still, his life was hectic, and he had to attend tea ceremonies or other social gatherings at his home or other places nearly every day. He also frequently traveled to other parts of the country to do exhibitions or attend other functions, often in Kyoto, so he had little time to himself. But it seemed that no matter how hard he worked to promote the school and the tea ceremony generally, powerful forces in the form of the new culture were working against him. The elegant old world that his family and his art came from were literally dying in front of him, and each year that passed was, in terms of revenue, worse than the last.

It wasn't that the tea ceremony and the other arts were not taught in schools. Indeed, they were still a part of every curriculum. It was just that the modern generation viewed them as entirely unnecessary, expensive (which they were), and worst of all, 'not fun.'

For the life of him, though, he couldn't understand why.

Today, he was already dressed in his usual black *kimono* and *hakama* (the pleated skirt worn over the *kimono*) as that afternoon he had to preside over yet another special tea ceremony for a politician friend and some visiting dignitaries from overseas in the main tearoom in the gardens.

This was nothing unusual for him, as the walls of his house would testify, being laden with framed pictures of himself and his late father with various famous people, quite a few of them presidents and prime ministers who had been visiting Japan and even some with the Emperor and other members of the Japanese royal family.

Mornings were his time though, his private space and the time of day when he could relax and read his newspaper in peace without the constant pressure of having to be somewhere or see someone. His wife and children rarely joined him, knowing he was even more irascible at this time of day than usual, and wisely took their breakfasts in the dining room and left him alone.

However, his quiet moment was over when the maid, a nice young girl called Eriko, came and told him that the builders wanted to see him.

"The builders?" he said in an annoyed voice. "What the hell do they want?"

"I don't know, *sensei*," said Eriko timidly. "They just asked for you to come and see something."

Takahashi threw his newspaper down, almost spilling his coffee in the process, and headed for the door as if ready for war. Like most people who occupied relatively high-level positions like his in the formal world of the old conservative Japanese society, he was intensely aware of his social status and fraternized as little with 'working people' as he possibly could. After all, what could they possibly understand about the rarefied world that *he* lived in? He remembered that his grandfather would not even answer a ringing telephone that sat on the table in front of him until his wife or some other servant came and did it for him. Yet now, he seemed to be at the beck and call of a construction crew. Obviously, this was a matter for his wife and not for him.

"Well, what is it?" he demanded when he saw Yusuke and his brother standing in the entranceway. "Is something wrong?"

Yusuke gave his brother a sideways look that implied 'Why did we bother?', and said in a business-like tone and without using the Grandmaster's correct title:

"We found this box in the wall of the tea house, Takahashi-san. Thought it might be something belonging to your family."

Takahashi glared at the dirty metal box at their feet.

"It looks like a piece of rubbish, if you ask me," he said.

"Right then. Shall we throw it out?" said Ichiro with a condescending smile.

18

"Yes, of course. Just throw it out," he said and turned rudely on his heel.

The men looked at each other, picked up the box, and left. They had done the right thing, but they were both surprised the old fellow didn't even want to have a look inside it, at least.

Maybe he had too much money anyway.

Takahashi was halfway down the hallway back to his newspaper and still fuming about whether these two idiots were going to ask him about every piece of junk they dug up when a nagging thought struck him.

"They found it in the wall?"

He stopped in his tracks.

Things had been found in the walls of tea houses before, old and valuable items that had been hidden away to keep them safe in more troubled times. The old plaster walls had often been used for storing things, partly because they were so simple to replace if needed.

He turned and went back to the doorway.

"Hey! Just a minute. Bring that back here," he shouted at the backs of the retreating men.

Yusuke and Ichiro turned and stared at him.

And in that simple moment, the seventeenth *iemoto* of the Takahashi School of The Japanese Tea Ceremony made one of the best decisions of his life.

About half an hour later, Eriko knocked on the sitting room door to see if he needed any more coffee, only to see something she had never thought to witness.

The master was sitting at the dining table in a profound reverie.

In front of him on the floor were the remains of an old metal box which he had prized open with a knife, and on the table was a little wooden box. The box, which was a filthy brown color and covered in mold and dust, was open, and an old blue cloth was lying next to it.

The *iemoto* was sitting with his head in his hands, staring at an old black tea bowl, almost as if he had never seen one like it before.

It was also quite clear that he had been crying.

Noticing her standing there, he turned and bellowed at her:

"Get OUT!"

Chapter 3

A Tea Lesson

Her cats found almost nothing more interesting than Penelope Middleton's fortnightly ritual of dressing herself in a *kimono* for her tea lesson. But whereas Coco, Biscuit, and Marmalade would content themselves with lining up at her bedroom door for the show, Alphonse knew it was his task to chase every piece of material that moved, especially when she wrapped the long silk belt around herself that held the whole thing together. That was altogether too much temptation for the black cat, who seemed to have confused the entire dressing exercise as a game designed specifically for his amusement.

As a (now retired) professor of Japanese literature who had lived in Kamakura for the last thirty-five years of her life, Penelope, or Penny-*sensei* as her many friends called her, was no stranger to *kimono*, and although it had taken her many years of sustained effort, she could dress herself from scratch in about thirty minutes, which was not a professional level speed, but it wasn't far off it either. Without Alphonse, she often mused, it might be even faster.

"Alphonse! You vile cat…" she hissed at him as the cat once again went for the end of her *obi,* but Alphonse was undeterred and continued his game of hooking his claws into the moving material and avoiding her reproving gaze with an air of unconcerned innocence.

"Ugh…" said Penelope, as she snatched it away from him once again.

Finally dressed, and with her shoulder-length silver hair swept up in an elegant bun, she checked her dress in the full-length mirror, which also displayed the four feline faces lined up behind her.

"Not too bad. It will have to do, anyway," she said out loud to her audience. Then she turned around and pointed a stern finger at Alphonse.

"No thanks to you," she reproved.

Alphonse gave a meow which meant, 'I don't know what you are talking about,' and trotted after her as she got ready to leave.

As she went downstairs into the living room, she saw her friend Fei coming in from the garden with some cherry tomatoes and aubergines in a little wicker basket.

"I don't think we are going to see any more of these this season," she said, putting the basket on the table. She looked up and gave Penelope's *kimono* a critical once over.

"Oh, are you wearing that one again?" she said, raising her eyebrows.

Penelope pouted.

"I *like* this one. It was one of Tanabe san's mother's *kimono*. She might be there today, I think."

The *kimono* was white silk with embroidered golden cranes, and she had teamed it with a light blue *obi* which also had a crane design.

"Looks like you are getting married," said Fei, referring to brides wearing a white *kimono* with crane designs.

"I will bear that in mind if ever I do," smiled Penelope, who, as most people knew, would rather have got bitten by a shark than enter the state of matrimony.

Fei laughed and went and sat in her usual old bamboo lounger overlooking the garden. She pulled out her long antique Japanese pipe and tobacco pouch and was soon emitting long plumes of smoke over the top of her beloved Asahi newspaper, which she unfailingly read from cover to cover each morning so she would be in a better position to unfurl her usual informed invective against the government of Japan, and particularly the ruling party, whom she loathed almost as much as she did organized religion.

Dr. Fei Chen was a former student of Penelope's at the nearby Hassei university. After graduation, she had succeeded in becoming the local police coroner, a position she still enjoyed today and which kept them all abreast of the latest in crime, which, while still relatively rare in Japan, still managed to keep the overstaffed police forces of the nation busy with its overwhelmingly minor cases, 95% of which involved traffic and bicycles.

Fei's family was of Chinese descent, her grandparents having immigrated to Japan before the War, and she lived in the house next door to Penelope's, where she looked after her elderly aunt, Auntie Chen. She had also never married and also never intended to. If she had a passion, apart from politics, it was the game of *shogi*, the Japanese form of chess, which she played at a very high level in one of the local clubs that was also patronized by several former and current police officers.

Penelope left her to her newspaper and, after farewelling her cats that had gathered at the doorway, made her way up the little street outside her old wooden house, stopping to say hello to several neighbors who, as usual, complimented her on her *kimono*. They all knew she went to her tea lesson every few weeks, and most of them also knew her teacher, Fujimoto-san, who lived just around the corner. Back when she was young, she had been very self-conscious and vividly remembered the stares she used to get being a foreigner wearing Japanese dress when she had first moved to this neighborhood, but now it had all become so normal both for them and for her that she barely gave how she looked a second thought. As far as she and her neighbors were concerned, she was as Japanese, if not more so, than them.

Penelope usually had her tea lessons at her teacher's house, where the old lady had a room dedicated to that; however, today, they had been invited to the Takahashi estate where they were renting one of the tea houses, which was something they occasionally did just for the sake of variety and also as an excuse to get together with a few old friends. Her teacher was also distantly related to the Takahashi family, having been a cousin of the Grandmaster's late first wife Sachiko, and had always maintained a close bond with Momoko, her daughter, who often came to their tea gatherings if she was free.

A short bus ride later, Penelope was standing in front of the front gates of the Takahashi estate, from whence she made her way up to the main house and around the side and through the gardens, where there was a short path leading to a small collection of tea houses. They were not allowed to use the main one, which was reserved for the *iemoto* and his family, but the next one along was theirs for the morning, and, as she bowed her way through the little *nijiriguchi* sliding door on her knees, she found her teacher and Momoko already laying out the utensils and getting the water in the kettle boiling.

"Oh, I'm glad you're here, Penny-*sensei*," said Momoko as the older woman settled herself next to her. "I've been wanting to see you. How is Dr. Chen?" she asked.

"She is as usual. I left her reading the newspaper in my living room. She thinks she owns my house too, you know."

Momoko, who was in her mid-twenties, looked beautiful as always, her shining black hair swept up and pinned with very expensive lacquer and gold comb, and she had chosen a simple crimson *kimono* with an autumn leaf design to reflect the coming of the season, which was just a few weeks away now. She had a small face, bright dark eyes, and a somewhat overly romantic nature with a tendency to fixate on things if they didn't seem right to her.

"Her father has been a perfect beast as usual," the elderly Fujimoto-san whispered, perhaps in case anyone was listening, which would have been highly unlikely.

"Why is that?" asked Penelope, as she helped herself to one of the sweets that had been left on a plate between them on the tatami mat floor.

"Oh, he's all wound up about tomorrow's *ochakai*. He keeps shouting at everyone and then changing his mind about everything. The gardener says he's quitting. Eriko, you know her, is terrified of him, and Haruko just stays in her room or goes out. I don't know where she goes…. I'm fed up," said Momoko.

An *ochakai*, or tea gathering, is a fairly common event in the tea world usually held to celebrate some major event, such as someone being granted a senior license, an award, or something else of that nature. Many guests are usually invited and were supposed to pay quite a bit for the honor of attending, so the school tended to be the primary beneficiary of these things.

Penny smiled understandingly. Everybody was well aware of the *iemoto's* rather difficult personality, and many were hoping for a change when his son, the mild-mannered Issei, eventually took over.

At this point, a few other ladies joined them, all old acquaintances, and Fujimoto-san, who was host today, made cups of thin tea for them and passed out some sweets she had ordered from her favorite sweet-maker in Kyoto.

"How many people are coming to the gathering tomorrow?" asked Yamada-san, another regular and rather elderly member of their little group.

Momoko waved her slender hand in the air in a gesture of desperation.

"I think he is having at least a few hundred or so. It's too big, I think. We haven't had such a big show since Grandfather retired. Also, he will not say what it's about, just that he will make a big announcement, and no one in the family is supposed to say anything. He's spent a pile of money on it, which we will never get back from the guests, and since he is always saying we are going bankrupt, it just makes no sense. You know he has invited Moribe-*sensei*?"

Penny raised her eyebrows. Moribe Yasuo had been a former Deputy Prime Minister at one point, as well as Foreign Minister before being deposed in a financial scandal some years previously. He was a well-known friend of the *iemoto's* late father, however. Penny didn't think it was so unusual, as indeed, it was not so uncommon for a Japanese politician to be involved in a financial scandal if it came to that.

"Well, it must be something important, I suppose. We will be there with bells on, won't we, ladies?" Penelope observed, and the other women who had all been invited to the event nodded. "I'm dying to hear what the old... what your father has up his sleeve," she said.

"*It had better be good, though,*" Penelope thought.

Momoko was right. These types of events were costly. If he was inviting people like Moribe to lend his name to it, you usually had to pay people like that a substantial sum to attend, whether or not they were friends of the family.

Momoko smiled and thanked them all.

"I'll just be glad when the whole thing is over," she opined.

After the thin tea course, Momoko took over as host to make the thick tea, which was prepared in a single large bowl passed from guest to guest.

Penelope always enjoyed watching Momoko make tea as the host. Being the daughter of a famous tea school *iemoto,* with a long and distinguished lineage, she had been expertly trained since birth in the art of the tea ceremony. Her every movement, from picking up the bamboo ladle to placing the kettle lid on the little ceramic rest, bespoke a timeless and effortless grace born of long practice. She was so naturally elegant that Penelope always felt like an elephant sitting beside her, and knew that she could never aspire to the skill level the young seemed to demonstrate so effortlessly.

"And how is young Issei-san these days?" Penelope asked. Momoko rolled her eyes.

"Still playing *mahjong* most nights, I think. He's promised to stay home with me tonight and watch a movie, though. He's hardly ever here otherwise. Neither is Haruko, she's always out as well. Which just leaves father and me here... I won't bother to tell you what that's like," she said with a downcast air.

Issei was Momoko's older brother and the heir to the title of *iemoto*. However, he had never seemed like he was ready for the role and spent most of his time drinking with his friends in Tokyo or playing mahjong in the clubs that had the prettiest hostesses. He and his father were well-known to be on terrible terms and barely spoke. Penelope and the others could scarcely remember the last time they had seen him in a tea room, but at least when he took over, things would probably be on a more even keel, as, for all his problems, Issei was a kind-hearted and easy-going young man whom everyone liked, and probably the exact opposite of his father.

Everyone said he took after his mother, the late Sachiko, who had been a great beauty and someone whom Penelope had known well. The advent of Haruko, whom the *iemoto* had married just a few years after her death, had come as quite a shock, as she was perhaps thirty years younger than her husband and more a contemporary of his daughter than his former wife. Nevertheless, Haruko had proved a charming person, and Penelope was glad that Momoko had someone like her in her life as it must have been a comfort having an ally in the house, which indeed she had proven to be.

After their tea lesson, Momoko walked them to the gate and wished them goodbye.

"I'm so pleased you are all coming tomorrow. It will be a relief to have you there," she said, giving them all a cheery wave goodbye.

Penelope and the rest of the women caught the bus back into town and had lunch together in a small Italian restaurant before they all headed their different ways home. They all agreed to meet at the same bus stop the following day, as they had all been asked to help prepare things for transport to the nearby Nikkei Hall, where the great *ochakai* was scheduled to be held.

"What on earth do you think this is all about?" asked Fujimoto-san as she walked with Penelope back through the familiar little streets in the direction of their homes.

"I have no idea. Do you think he is going to announce his retirement?" asked Penelope.

"Hmmm… I'm not sure. I don't think he thinks Issei is ready yet. Probably the old fool will carry on for another ten years or so yet."

They arrived at Fujimoto-san's front door, and her old teacher asked her in for tea, but Penelope politely declined.

"I think I've done more than enough tea for one day. I will see you tomorrow. I think it's going to be a long day…" she said.

A few minutes later, she was home. All four of her cats were lined up inside in the entranceway again waiting for her and, no doubt, dinner. Fei seemed to have returned to her own house, no doubt to tend to her aunt. She now worked part-time as a coroner, so she only came in if the police called her for something, which meant she had much more free time than before.

Penelope also had been challenged when she retired from the university three years ago. She had been a full-time professor until the last day, and her life had been extremely busy between lecturing, grading, seeing students and a myriad of administrative matters.

However, she still had her writing and made it a point to turn out a decent amount of work each day according to a schedule she set for whatever project she was working on. She had written and edited several books on Japanese literature and dozens of articles during her long career, but her true love had always been translation. She had translated several Japanese writers into English, including some of the younger generations who seemed to be getting quite a reputation overseas now thanks to her and she had also become quite sought after by various publishers wanting her skills in this regard. Mainly, however, she was interested in translating older writers, the old poets of the later Edo Period, and she tended to specialize in these instead of the more lucrative current-day authors.

Finally out of her *kimono*, which was always a relief, she sat in her much more comfortable western clothes on the little wooden verandah of her house overlooking her beloved garden, which was now almost wholly dedicated to growing vegetables and herbs, something which she and Fei enjoyed working on together. She cut up some watermelon from the refrigerator and sat eating it with Alphonse curled next to her. The other cats were nowhere to be seen, though they were probably to be found enjoying the late afternoon sunshine in their favorite haunts somewhere in the garden.

Sitting there in the fading sunlight, she thought about the Takahashi family. Something about them gave her an ill feeling whenever she went there. She liked Momoko well enough, but the rest of the family seemed so concentrated on either making or spending money that it made her shudder quietly. It seemed somehow quite perverse to her that the tea ceremony, which she loved, seemed to have degenerated into a commercial enterprise at the hands of the big schools, who seemed to care nothing for the original purpose other than how it generated a whopping income from their many students, who not only paid for lessons but for all the various 'licenses' that the schools had dreamed up over the years in order to make even more money.

It had not always been so crassly commercial, though. She had once translated a biography of Sen no Rikyu, the founder of the tea ceremony in the sixteenth century, for a publishing company and found it quite illuminating. Compared to the big tea schools, which all traced their roots back to him in one way or another, Rikyu's idea of tea had been simplicity itself. His rules, of which there were only a dozen or so, included such things as to arrange the flowers as though they were in the field, to be ready ahead of time, and, her favorite, to be prepared in case it should rain. There were basically no instructions as to how the ceremony was to be done, unlike today, where it would take literally a lifetime to learn all the procedures that had been cooked up, with most of these dating from just after the War.

Instead, Rikyu saw the ceremony as a form of quiet meditation, a way of being in the moment with others and finding beauty in the humble and everyday implements used to perform the simple function of making a bowl of tea and enjoying its taste.

She often reminded herself of these ideas when she went to these grand events such as those promised tomorrow, and she knew that in her own quiet practice with her friends, they were much closer to old Rikyu's ideas.

And with them, she found a great deal of happiness.

Chapter 4.

A Death in the Family

The morning of the great day was bright and clear. It was also very warm even by 8 am when she and Fujimoto-san and several of the others met up at the bus stop for the short ride to the Takahashi estate, which was such a local landmark that the bus stop in front of it was even named *'Takahashimae'* or 'in front of Takahashi' after the place.

Kamakura, being a seaside town, was usually a few degrees cooler in September than the sweltering capital, however, it was going to be another exhaustingly humid day today according to the weather forecast, as was also indicated by the sound of the cicadas singing in the trees, which was almost deafening at times. It was certainly not the weather to be wearing a heavy silk *kimono*, and all the ladies had their fans out and were praying the air-conditioned bus would be along soon before they all turned into puddles, as Fujimoto-san put it.

The five women were all dressed in one of their better (or even best) *kimono*, and all of them carried small bundles of tea equipment they were bringing to the occasion tied up in traditional silk *furoshiki* wrapping cloths. As expected, the focus of their conversation revolved around the mysterious purpose of today's *ochakai*, and they were all naturally longing to find out what it was all about. Penelope felt it was rather like being asked to go to Bilbo's famous birthday party in a way, but she kept that rather literary reference to herself.

'I'm just hoping he's not retiring right now," chimed Ibara-san, who had known the Takahashi family since the time of the grandfather's ascension to the *iemoto* title. "That boy is not ready yet, not by a long shot."

The others agreed with her, and there was yet another rehash of Issei's character, which lasted until they reached their destination. Penelope, who even though she was now in her mid-sixties was still the youngest of the group, had to admit that even though the young man was good-looking, well-mannered, and had an easy charm, she had always had a bad feeling about him, ever since she had first met him as a child, which was a feeling she also shared with several of her friends.

It was a well-known fact that the first-born sons of prominent families involved in the traditional Japanese arts like tea and stage arts, such as *noh* and *kabuki*, had their paths in life mapped out for them from the moment of their birth. Children like Issei were well-educated at the most elite schools, but there was absolutely no question as to where their future lay, which was to follow in the footsteps of their ancestors and fulfil their roles. But they were also often incredibly spoilt, and Issei had been no exception.

Despite his often lackadaisical approach to his studies in the tea ceremony, he was a more than proficient practitioner and had a fair bit of technical and historical knowledge to boot, as she had seen demonstrated on the rare occasions his skills had been put on display in the past.

That being said, he was far below the level of his beautiful younger sister Momoko, who had always devoted her whole heart to the art and knew a great deal more than her brother, who spent most of his time now partying with his friends in Tokyo.

Recently, and much to the disgust of his father, but perhaps also to impress these same friends, he had used some of the money from his grandfather's bequest to fund the purchase of a very flashy red vintage Porsche, which as the air to a title in the tradition-soaked and highly conservative world of the tea ceremony was a faux pas of the first water.

You may be rich, but you shouldn't ever flaunt it, was rule number one in this country, as any businessman could tell you.

Having completed their short ride, the women entered the estate via the massive old iron gates at the entrance to the property, which, if you looked closely, had an ornate 'T' as part of their design. However, as they started up the driveway towards the main house this morning, Penelope and some of the others began to sense that something was not quite right.

The first thing they noticed was that several of the staff were rushing around and shouting, and then they saw a group of other people running in the direction of the tea houses in the gardens to the side of the house.

As the women got closer, Penelope also noticed that the small door to the main tea house was open, and there was now a crowd of people around it. She then saw Momoko, dressed in a dark blue *kimono* come running back from the tea house towards the house, and that she was obviously distraught. She was followed by Issei, walking slowly with a somber look on his face. He cast the women a quick glance and then walked after his sister into the house without further acknowledgment.

The women all exchanged surprised glances and stopped in their tracks in the driveway, unsure whether to proceed or not.

At this point, Penelope noticed Eriko, the Takahashi's maid, sitting on a little bench not far from them. The girl was slumped forward with her head in her hands and weeping.

Penelope, who lived in the same street and knew her and her family well, sat down next to her and put her arm around her shoulders.

In response, the girl looked up at her, pointed a shaking hand at the main tea house where the crowd of staff had gathered, and said in a quaking voice:

"He's dead. In there... The master..."

Penelope shot a glance at the tea house.

"How? What on earth happened?" she asked the shaken girl, whose whole body was trembling.

Eriko shook her head.

"I don't know. He wasn't in the house this morning. No one could find him, so I went to the tea house, but the door was locked. I thought I should just check anyway.... There was no answer when I knocked, so I used my key. He was on the floor...."

"Did someone call an ambulance?" Penelope asked.

Eriko shook her head again.

"I suppose so…" she quavered.

Penelope gave the girl a few words of comfort, but then her curiosity got the better of her, and she walked towards the tea house. In the distance, she heard the sounds of a siren, which was either an ambulance or the police or both. She knew she would have to be quick.

She eased herself past one of the gardeners kneeling at the little doorway to the house and peered inside.

The first thing she saw was the *iemoto*, lying on his side on the tatami mat floor, his mouth open and a look of horror in his unmoving eyes. Even from the doorway, she could tell he was clearly dead.

He was still dressed in his usual black formal *kimono* and *hakama*, and he seemed to have collapsed face forward on the floor with one arm stretched out as if reaching for a black tea bowl that lay on its side on the floor just out of reach.

Penelope slid into the room on her knees and quickly glanced around.

The first thing she saw was that the room seemed to be set up for a tea ceremony. Why this would strike her as odd, she could not say, but there was somehow something incongruous about the whole scene, rather like she had walked onto a film set or like something which had been prearranged to look like a tea ceremony.

The lid for the iron kettle sat on its small ceramic rest, and beside it there was a small black tea container, a waste water bowl, a white *hagi* ware container for the water, and also a small bamboo tea scoop and a bamboo whisk, which was lying on its side a few feet away from the body. The bamboo ladle, the *hishaku*, was also sitting correctly balanced on its little rest as if it had just been used to draw the water to add to the bowl. Everything you needed to conduct a ceremony was laid out in the correct fashion, perfectly placed, and organized.

A seasoned practitioner herself, Penelope could see at a glance what stage of the ceremony the master had been at when he died, which would have been the moment when the guests would have drunk from the bowls of tea that had been prepared.

Except there was only one person here, so presumably the *iemoto* had been making tea for his own pleasure.

She bent down next to the metal brazier holding the iron kettle. The coals underneath it were still warm, as was the side of the kettle when she held her hand close to it.

Penelope was intrigued. The *iemoto* had obviously been engaged in a private ceremony of his own at the time he died, which, judging from the lack of heat on the kettle, had been sometime during the previous evening.

At that moment, she heard the sound of feet running towards the tea house, and a few seconds later, a white-helmeted ambulance man poked his head through the little door and stared at her.

Penelope stood, beckoned the man to come inside, and moved to one side with her back against the wall. The man hurriedly entered without even removing his shoes and crouched over the body, feeling for a pulse with two fingers at the carotid vein at the neck. He stopped after a moment, and another ambulance man entered and bent at his side. The second man also stared at her for a moment, and Penelope, in a sudden flash of self-awareness, grasped how strange it must look for these men to see a dead body on the floor of a tea house with a foreigner in *kimono* standing over it.

"Time to go," she thought.

Penelope bowed her head to leave via the little *nijiriguchi* doorway, and as she did so, she reached out her hand to the door frame to steady herself and accidentally touched the old light switch on the wall. For some reason, it occurred to her that even though she had been in this room several times before, she had never noticed this switch, which struck her as odd for some reason.

She emerged once more into the sunlight and was met by more paramedics at the doorway, some of whom were busy setting up a stretcher. She also noticed three police officers running towards the house from their cars which had been hastily parked in the driveway.

Penelope made her way back to her friends, who had been standing waiting and who were quite shocked at seeing her boldness in entering the tea house while at the same time desperate to know what she had seen.

"He's dead," Penelope said quietly.

"Oh my God..." said Fujimoto-san, raising her hand to her mouth.

At that moment, Momoko appeared by the doorway of the house, and the women gathered around her, expressing their condolences.

She was still very shaken, but she had dried her tears and was trying to compose herself for what she knew now lay ahead.

"I just can't believe it. We all had dinner together last night, well, Haruko wasn't there, but he seemed fine. He was even in a good mood for once. Issei is hardly ever there for dinner, maybe that was why, I don't know," she looked around at them miserably as if looking for an answer.

"Where is Haruko san now? Does she know?" asked Fujimoto-san, who of all the women knew Momoko best.

The girl nodded her head.

"She's in her room. Issei told her what happened. She said she didn't want to see... him...."

The women looked at each other, and Penelope knew at once what they were thinking. What wife would not run to see her husband if he had just died?

"That seems a bit odd..." said Ibara-san, who was quickly silenced by a few of the other women.

"We all grieve in our own way..." said Fujimoto-san. "Just let her be. It must have been a dreadful shock."

Momoko nodded again.

"I guess we need to cancel this *ochakai*," she said. "I better talk to Issei about it."

The women nodded and told her they would stay and help with anything she needed.

Two more squad cars now arrived, and at the same time, a large fire engine parked itself outside the gates. It seemed that once you called the emergency services, everything turned up whether you needed it or not, which was rather typical of the way things worked in Japan, where a response that was not total was seen as somehow lacking in the appropriate effort.

Penelope was not surprised to see the familiar face of her friend Fei getting out of one of the squad cars, but Fei seemed quite surprised to see her.

"What are you doing here? Oh… that's right… the *ochakai*… that was today, wasn't it? I'd forgotten…" she said.

Fei was dressed in her 'work' clothes, which consisted of slacks and a blazer with her usual white coroner's coat and black medical bag.

Penelope nodded.

"They told you who it was?" she asked.

Fei nodded and, taking her arm, drew her aside from the others.

"He's in there?" she asked, nodding towards the tea house, which was surrounded by police and ambulance people.

"Yes. I saw him," Penelope confessed.

Fei smiled. "I knew you couldn't resist. So you disturbed a potential crime scene? That figures."

Penelope blushed. "I did no such thing. I just looked. And left. A minute, that was all…" she asserted sternly. "Why do you say it's a crime scene, anyway?"

Fei was always teasing her for one reason or the other.

"You never know, do you? Who found him?" she asked.

"Probably Eriko-san, I think," said Penelope, nodding towards the bench where the still distraught girl was sitting.

Fei glanced at her. "Poor thing. I've known her since she was a kid. Anyway… work. See you later," she said and headed for the tea house, swinging her black bag.

Fei was a no-nonsense and extremely thorough professional who had absolutely zero tolerance for fools of any kind, something which had gained her a somewhat fearsome reputation in the police force, which had no shortage of them, it seemed. She was slender and wore her hair short like a man (in fact, she even used a cheap men's barber) and wore her glasses on a beaded chain around her neck, which she had a habit of peering over at you if she had something to say.

Penelope found it interesting that even though Fei had been born in Japan, she had none of the usual Japanese 'indirect' fussiness about her. Instead, she had a much more direct 'Chinese' personality, almost like she had just stepped off the boat from Shanghai. Penelope attributed this mainly to her parents and also to her aunt, the elderly and quite infamous Auntie Chen, who was the terror of every small shopkeeper in Kamakura for her unhesitating criticism of any goods or services she deemed not up to her standards, and had been known to berate her unfortunate victims for upwards of an hour should they dare to talk back to her.

Penelope walked back to where her friends were now sitting and comforting Eriko on the bench. She didn't want to say anything, but she had the definite feeling that something was amiss with the scene in the tea house she had just witnessed, and it was beginning to nag at her.

"Eriko-san, did Takahashi *sensei* often go to the tea house by himself?" she asked.

The startled girl looked up at her, slightly bewildered.

"I... I don't know. Sometimes. Yes. Recently he was often in there...," she replied.

"Do you know why?"

The girl shook her head.

"I don't know. He keeps a lot of stuff in there. That's why we lock it," she said.

Penelope nodded.

Usually, tea houses did not have actual locks like other buildings and just had sliding wooden doors, yet it could be expected here that they had a little more security, especially if they kept anything valuable in there, which was quite likely in a place like this. The Takahashi School, she knew, had a very fine collection of old tea bowls and scrolls and other items made by master craftsmen over the centuries, which would have easily run into the tens of millions of yen. Penelope even knew several tea connoisseurs like the Takahashi family who kept their most expensive things in strong boxes at a bank and only brought them out for special occasions.

"And the door was locked when you found him?" she asked.

"Yes. I told you, I used my key. I just wanted to see if there was anything wrong...."

Penelope stared at the tea house. The image of the *iemoto* lying there, his face contorted in pain, filled her mind. He had been making tea. Why had he been doing that?

"And why did you lock the door?" she whispered to herself.

Chapter 5

Conspiracy Theories

One of the joys of living in Japan, or indeed anywhere, is to have a local restaurant where people know you and look forward to seeing you, where the food is good and the atmosphere relaxing and you can take a break from cooking and relax with the people you like.

For Penelope Middleton, that kind of place also had to be somewhere where she could indulge her favorite vices: sake, and its companion, *yakitori*, or skewered grilled chicken. Her favorite place for this, and where she could be found at least twice a week and invariably in the company of Fei, was a small *yakitori* restaurant in the main shopping street of Kamakura owned by the Yamazaki family, a place she had patronized for nearly thirty years.

Fei had been the one who introduced her to the Yamazaki family restaurant all those many years ago, as she absolutely loved sake and *yakitori* herself, and she probably went there more often than Penelope.

Even though the pair would no doubt have raised a lot of eyebrows in most Japanese establishments, the locals who went here were so completely used to the pipe-smoking doctor and her foreign professor friend that they never gave them a sideways glance. This could have been in part because they were both fiercely protected by the Yamazaki family, particularly the acerbic wife, Kazuko, who had been known to throw drunk customers out on their ear for daring to bother her regulars, and that particularly meant Penelope and Fei, who actually could have stood up for themselves quite well had they ever been given the chance.

Penelope was a rare enough commodity all on her own, though. She had been the only female professor of Japanese literature on the campus when she was first hired, as well as the first foreign academic the university had ever employed, so she was used to getting a lot of attention from everybody. Over the years, however, as her language skills had improved and as she adapted to the Japanese way of life, she found herself not even noticing if people looked at her differently. She also found that, oddly enough, when she stopped caring, usually so did they.

Tonight being a Friday, Fei and Penelope were at their usual table at the back of the restaurant indulging in their first flask of sake and deep in conversation with Kazuko and her husband Hiro over the recent events at the Takahashi estate.

Over the past week, and as was customary in Japan, where funerals were held quickly after a death, things had been moving swiftly.

After someone dies in Japan, the funeral usually has two or three stages rather than just one.

The first was the *otsuya*, or the vigil. This took place shortly after the death, often on the following evening, and then on the next day there would be a ceremony at a funeral parlor where the body would be cremated. Burials were still extremely rare in Japan due to a lack of land but mainly because it was the tradition, and in the case of funerals, tradition trumped everything else.

In the case of the *iemoto*, The funeral arrangements had been delayed due to the nature of the death, and were held a few days later than usual as soon as the body had been released from Dr. Chen's care at the police mortuary.

Both Fei and Penelope had attended the *otsuya* at the main house on the estate, where they had prayed and offered incense before a large picture of the deceased placed on an easel and surrounded by an array of the traditional chrysanthemums, which were the flower associated with death and the next life. Momoko and the rest of the family had been there, of course, and also there had been a constant stream of hundreds of other people, not only from the tea world but also from the other Japanese arts as well as quite a number of well-known celebrities, politicians and the like.

Momoko greeted them and thanked them for coming, whereas Haruko and Issei just sat in their seats and stared straight ahead, barely acknowledging anyone unless they made direct eye contact. There was something cold about both of them that Penelope and others had noticed before, as if the rest of the world were beneath their attention.

The funeral had been held at Kencho-ji temple the next day and, according to the family's wishes, it was a private affair, and the public and the media had been kept away.

Naturally enough, there had been a lot of attention from the media, as the *iemoto* had been a very well-known figure, and although the cause of death was not known to them yet, the fact that it had been a suicide had soon become public knowledge, and this had lit up the TV networks like a Christmas tree. The local police had even posted an officer outside of the gates of the estate as a courtesy to keep them away, and there were still reporters and camera crews hanging around even a week later.

Tonight the usual folk were at the Yamazaki's restaurant, a small place with only four tables and a bar where about five more could sit, and where the TV on the wall was perennially fixed on the baseball channel.

"So are you going to tell us?" asked Kazuko as she delivered them a plate of steaming yakitori. "Or do I have to wait for Shukan Fuji?" she demanded, citing one of Japan's most notorious gossip magazines.

Hiro was also listening with one ear cocked as he stood, turning the yakitori sticks over his charcoal grill.

Fei took a sip of sake and smiled mischievously.

"This could be a little colder, don't you think?" she said, waving her glass at him.

Kazuko sat down at their table and, folding her arms, gave her an irritated stare.

"Alright, alright... I'll tell you," said Fei, "It's going to be public knowledge anyway very soon, but don't go shouting it around, alright?"

"My lips are sealed," said Kazuko, who was one of the biggest gossips in Kamakura.

"I'm sure," said Penelope rolling her eyes.

Fei looked at them both.

"He poisoned himself. Cyanide. It was a pretty quick death," she said in a low voice.

Kazuko put her hand to her mouth.

"Seriously?" she whispered.

"Seriously," said Penelope, who had already heard the story from her friend.

"No… I don't believe it," said Hiro from the bar. "He'd never do that. He was way too up himself," he said rather rudely.

Kazuko gave him a terse stare.

"He has a point, though," she said.

"How so?" asked Penelope.

"He just never struck me as the type. You know. He was rich. Huge house. Hobnobbed with politicians. Knew the Emperor even. Everyone knew him. Why would he do that?"

"Yep. Someone bumped him off for sure," said her husband.

"Well, maybe not. He had a lot of financial issues, for a starter," said Fei.

Penelope nodded.

"It's true, Momoko was telling me just the day before he was worried about bankruptcy," she said.

Kazuko stared at her in surprise.

"What? Him? Bankrupt?... What about the boy and his new sportscar?"

Penelope smiled at how Kazuko seemed to always know everything that happened in Kamakura.

"Grandad's money. Not the papa's," she said. "Papa would never buy him such a toy. It's the wrong… optics, I think people say these days."

Fei lit her pipe and blew a stream of smoke at the ceiling.

"That's for sure," she said with a wry smile.

Kazuko stood up and went to serve a group of office workers who had just arrived and left them alone for a while.

"I think Hiro has a point, too," she said to Fei seriously as she slid some yakitori from the skewer with her chopsticks and made a little pile on the plate.

Fei tossed back her sake and gave her an amused look.

"This could *definitely* be colder, Hiro!" she held up the sake flask and shouted at the chef.

"*Hai*," said Hiro without looking up from the grill.

"Why would you say that?" she said, giving Penelope an amused smile. "Don't tell me you are turning into one of those conspiracy theorists in your old age."

"Well, the *door* for a start," said Penelope leaning forward and lowering her voice.

"The door? What about it?"

"It was locked."

"So?"

"So why would he lock the door?" asked Penelope.

Fei waved the empty flask at Hiro.

"Can I have a cold one, *please*? And a glass of beer. I'd like *that* cold too…."

Hiro gave her a glass and a bottle of Kirin lager.

"I put the sake in the fridge. You'll have to wait a minute," he said as he returned to his grill.

Fei smiled. "You are a good man, Hiro."

"I know," he grunted.

She turned to Penelope.

"Look, this is easy. He locked the door because he was going to top himself and wanted some privacy," she said in English, perhaps so no one else would understand.

49

They usually spoke to each other in Japanese, but Fei's English was also excellent, and this had become a sort of secret language between them when they didn't want to be overheard. Fei was also very fond of British slang, which she usually got upside down, but phrases like 'top yourself' were among her favorites.

Penelope gave her a long look.

"Or someone locked him in there because they didn't want the body to be found until later."

"Oh, come on, Penny...." Fei laughed.

"I'm serious. And why poison? Why would anybody kill themselves that way?"

"Why? Because it's quick for a start. There was enough poison in that tea to kill six people. He was probably dead before he hit the floor," said Fei.

Penelope was silent for a moment.

"It doesn't fit," she said

"What doesn't fit?" said Fei as she helped herself to some chicken.

Penelope raised her glass and stared at it as she swirled the sake slightly.

"If I were a tea master... I would do it the old-fashioned way," she said.

Fei gave her a surprised look. "What? Do you mean *seppuku*? Be serious."

Seppuku was ritual suicide, where the person would spread out a white sheet, write a final poem and then bare their stomach and perform the act of cutting open the belly, or *hara-kiri*, to release the soul from the body. This was usually done with an assistant standing by, who would instantly strike off the person's head with a sword, thus sparing them a long and agonizing death.

"Well, maybe not *seppuku*, but he would certainly write a death poem. He was a tea master, Fei. And he was quite a showboater as well. Think about it. He goes into his tea house. He makes a final cup of tea. It's all so... ritualistic. No one like him would commit suicide without leaving a death poem. That would be completely out of character, I think."

"Just bring the sake, Hiro. I can't wait any longer," Fei shouted.

After Hiro returned with a fresh flask, Fei poured them two glasses.

"Actually, he did leave something. He left a letter."

"Really?"

"Yes. Do you want to see it? And DON'T tell anyone I showed it to you."

Penelope nodded as Fei fished in her little rucksack and found her phone. She then showed her a photograph of the document in question, which was a one-line email.

Penelope read it aloud in a low voice.

"I'm sorry to have caused many people trouble. Goodbye."

She passed the phone back to Fei.

"That's not a death poem. That's something politicians write when they resign after being caught with their hands in the till. No tea master would write that," she said. "That just makes me more suspicious, not less."

"It's from his computer and his email account," intoned her friend.

"Who did he send it to?"

"His family, I guess. The three of them. Momoko, Issei and Haruko."

"Seriously? And what would you do if you suddenly got a mail like this? Wouldn't you rush out and find him?"

"That's a point, I would. Except he never sent it. He printed it and left it on his desk," Fei said with a triumphant smile.

Penelope shook her head. "I don't buy it. And now I've seen this, I doubt I ever will."

"You're turning into one of those nutters who believe in aliens," said Fei finishing half her large glass of beer in one hit, which was something that Penelope always marveled anyone could do, but Fei's ability to drink just about anyone under the table was the stuff of considerable legend in the area.

Penelope laughed.

"OK, explain this. Who organizes a huge *ochakai* and invites two hundred people, including a pile of 'dignitaries' for lack of a better word, in order to make some big announcement, and then kills himself the night before? That's like not turning up for your own birthday party. I guess it might explain the note, though…."

"Yeah, OK," said Fei shrugging and lighting her pipe again. "That's a point. You tell me…"

"No, you tell me. Momoko said he was in a great mood the night before. He was obviously looking forward to the big reveal. And then he tops himself in the tearoom and leaves a one-line email like this?" she pointed to Fei's phone on the table.

"Maybe Momoko didn't know her papa as well as she thinks," said Fei.

52

"Given this, I doubt anybody did."

They were silent for a minute.

"Anyway, there was no evidence of anyone else in that room. Just him. He wasn't making tea for anyone else. He was having his own little party…." said Fei.

"Hmmm… I know it's quite normal to make tea just for yourself, but it always feels kind of sad. Tea is meant to be shared in a sense. Why make your last act so lonely? Usually, in the past, when people committed suicide, they would have a little party beforehand for their friends. They would eat and drink, and then the person would write a final poem. I still don't see why he didn't do that," said Penelope.

Fei laughed. "Look, it's not the eighth century, you know. You've been reading too much *Tale of Genji*, professor. Anyway, there was no one else there. Only one bowl of tea was found."

"Maybe," said Penelope, still lost in her thoughts. "Unless they cleaned up after themselves…."

Kazuko suddenly sat down beside Penelope and lit a cigarette.

"So, who do you think did it?" she asked with a serious look at them.

Fei rolled her eyes. "No one did it. He did it. You are getting as bad as her."

Kazuko gave Penelope a dig in the ribs and smiled.

"Great minds think alike."

"No, perverted minds think alike," laughed Fei "it's just a better story for you guys to spread around that he was murdered by Jack the Ripper or something. The door was locked. Only him in the room. End of story. Sorry."

Kazuko, an inveterate watcher of mystery dramas on TV, immediately found a flaw in Fei's analysis.

"Did he have the only key? Did they find the key on him?"

"Oh, for God's sake, what is this, *Friday Night Hot Spring Murder*?" said Fei with a laugh, referring to a popular TV series. "No, he didn't have the only key. The maid had one, and another was hanging up in the kitchen. And yes, they found his key inside. Satisfied?"

"So they could have killed him and locked him in there so they could find the body later, right?"

Penelope nodded.

"See, Penny *sensei* agrees with me," said Kazuko with a wink at Penelope.

"You both watch too much TV," Said Fei.

Penelope poured a glass of sake for Kazuko. "Actually, you know quite well I hardly ever watch TV. Kazuko san watches it for me."

She and Kazuko clinked glasses.

"What's this about money problems, anyway? I thought they were stinking rich?" asked Kazuko

"Apparently not so rich, according to Momoko. I don't think the tea business is quite what it used to be," said Penelope.

"So, what will happen to the school?" she asked.

"Well, I expect Issei will become *iemoto*. That's what usually happens in these instances, I think," said Penelope.

"Issei? I doubt that boy knows one side of a tea bowl from another. I hear he prefers gambling up in Tokyo. He's pretty well known around the hostess bars, my friends tell me."

"That's what I've heard, too," said Penelope.

"I guess it will make Momoko's life easier," said Kazuko. "Her father was a total pig; that's what everyone says. Anyway, they must have pots of money. That property is worth a mint, and they have a lot of super expensive stuff, I bet. Probably Issei will lose the lot at the track by the end of the month."

Penelope and Fei laughed, and the three of them clinked classes again and ordered more sake.

When they were alone again later in the evening, Penelope still had death on her mind.

"You know, there is one more thing that's been bothering me."

"OK…" said Fei. "I'm waiting…."

"When I was leaving the tea house, you know when the ambulance guys were coming in, I put my hand on the wall when I was going through the *nijiriguchi* and touched the light switch. I'd never even noticed it before, I guess, because I've only ever been in there during the day. I mean, who does tea at night?"

Fei looked at her inquiringly.

"So?"

"So it was one of those old-fashioned light switches, you know, the ones that are a bit hard to turn on and off."

"And…" said Fei.

"And I noticed the light was turned off."

Fei laughed.

"So? It was the middle of the morning."

"I know. But tell me this. Who commits suicide in a dark room?" asked Penelope.

Chapter 6

Shogi Night

Penelope had always thought it incongruous that her typically impatient and unconventional friend Fei should be so in love with *shogi*, the Japanese version of chess.

It seemed an odd choice of hobby for her, as *shogi* was a game not just of strategy but also of nerves and especially of patience. In the professional leagues at high levels, a single game could go on for a whole day, and players, dressed in formal *kimono* and sitting upright on cushions in the formal *seiza* position could spend upwards of an hour contemplating a single move. Whenever she saw professional *shogi* on television, she would think of her friend and wonder what on earth it was that drew her so to the game. So slow, so conservative, and so intensely *Japanese...* and so unlike *her.*

Nevertheless, Fei had enjoyed a lifetime passion for the game, which had always teetered on an obsession, ever since a teacher at her primary school had suggested she come along to the school's *shogi* club one afternoon. She had taken a liking to the game more or less instantly and, in a few months, was beating all the other students. She then started taking lessons at the headquarters of the *shogi* association in

Ichigaya in central Tokyo, where she was instantly recognized as a prodigy and quickly shot up the ranks and began winning tournaments in her age group.

When she had been a teenager and already at the second *dan* level, she had even horrified her parents with the thought of turning professional rather than following a career in medicine. In the end, she had chosen to keep her parents happy, but even without following her dreams to be a professional, she was a highly ranked amateur player in the women's leagues in Japan and still played in the occasional tournament, where she had often triumphed over professional players. There was even a picture of her she kept framed on the wall of her house of a match she played against Habu Yoshihara, probably the most celebrated *shogi* player of the last several decades. It was a game she had lost, but barely.

These days, apart from studying the game in her free time, which she duly did almost every day, Fei mainly played with other police officers at a *shogi* club in the town, where her usual opponent was Chief Inspector Yamashita, who was of a similar rank to her own in the men's league.

The two had been opponents for over twenty years, and once a month, the bachelor inspector came to her house for dinner and to play, which was where Penelope had got to know him as well.

The Chief Inspector was a quiet, intense man with a soft voice and a precise and extremely polite way of speaking to you that could come across as quite cold. However, once he got to know you and relaxed, he was warm and very friendly, albeit in a formal and quite intellectual manner.

He lived alone in his old family home in the north part of Kamakura near the famous Engakuji temple, where his older brother was now head monk and was thus slated to be the next abbot in the future. His family was an old Zen Buddhist family, and many of its members had been either lay priests or clergy down through the centuries. The inspector himself had gone to one of the major universities that trained people for the Buddhist priesthood before changing to become a law student in his second year and later joining the police.

Penelope had always felt that he would have been a natural as a monk though, as there was something so profoundly tranquil about him that she and probably many others found soothing. Still, he was a deeply intellectual man and valued a life where he could use his gifts to protect others, despite the many virtues of life as a priest.

On meeting him, it was clear that he was most comfortable alone, and in fact, he tended to spend his free time reading and also writing, an interest he shared with Penelope. He was the author of several books on different topics, a few of which were even very well-crafted mystery novels that Penelope had read with enjoyment.

He had also been bitten by the *shogi* bug as a young child, having been taught the game by his uncle, who had also been a Zen priest at another monastery in Fukui Prefecture. Like Fei, he had also quickly developed into a highly competitive player and was known for his fierce and quite abandoned style of play, which was why Fei, who played in a very similar way herself, clearly enjoyed their games.

About a week after their dinner at their usual *yakitori* restaurant, it happened to be the night of his monthly visit to the house Fei shared with her aunt, the redoubtable Auntie Chen. Since he was also the officer in charge of the Takahashi case, which had not yet been officially ruled a suicide nor a death by foul play, Penelope seized on the chance to learn more about the latest developments in the case.

When she arrived, the pair had just finished setting up the *shogi* board on the dining room table after Auntie Chen's usually colossal feast. Whenever she or Fei had guests, Auntie Chen, who had immigrated from Shanghai in the 50s with her parents and had never forgotten her Chinese heritage, bombarded them with an ocean of food that usually left people unable to eat for days afterward. The old woman still spoke the language fluently, which Fei did not, had many Chinese friends and relatives and kept her house in the traditional Chinese fashion, with a large round table in the living room redolent of a Chinese restaurant and with Chinese art and furniture and various knickknacks everywhere. She also cooked only Chinese food ("not that Japanese stuff, bad for health") and drank only tea, which she imported directly from a relative in Taiwan.

When Auntie Chen cooked you a meal, it was usually several courses, and there was absolutely no saying 'no' to more food when it was offered. Penelope, therefore, usually came over after dinner rather than suffer through yet another force-feeding at her hands.

Fortunately, despite his athletic frame, the Chief Inspector was a gourmet and loved Chinese food, so he always enjoyed his visits to Auntie Chen, who he always complimented as a superb cook. He was a reasonably decent chef in his own right, but he always said that as a bachelor, he didn't feel motivated to go to a lot of fuss just for himself and lived on a relatively spartan and traditional Japanese diet that would not have been unusual at his brother's monastery.

This evening as Penelope entered, Auntie Chen was busy in the kitchen washing the dishes, and thus she escaped the usual comments about how she was 'looking thin" and needed to "eat more." She still got this advice even though she was already a bit overweight and knew she needed to do something about it, but she couldn't bring herself to give anything up, especially sake.

The inspector rose from his seat and bowed to her in his usual formal way as he always did, and Penelope sat down at the dining table with them to watch them play. They had just started their game, and she knew they would be playing for at least a couple of hours as they never rushed their moves and played casually without a timer.

Auntie Chen arrived with a large cup of jasmine tea and a plate of snacks. The TV was on in the corner of the room with one of the many romantic Korean soap operas that Auntie Chen was addicted to, and Penelope found herself watching them out of her eye and wondering, as usual, why no one ever kissed.

The inspector was sitting back with his arms folded, waiting for Fei to move, and was dressed as usual in a dark suit. However, he had dispensed with his tie, which was neatly folded in his jacket pocket in a nod to being off work.

"Have you just come from the station?" Penelope asked him.

The inspector nodded.

"Yes, it's been pretty busy lately. My desk is full of personnel reports I have to update by the end of the week and a lot of other nonsense for the powers that be. Sometimes I wish I had just stayed as a sergeant. It would have been a lot easier…."

"Yes, I can imagine," said Penelope consolingly.

Fei made her move, which caused the inspector to raise his eyebrows.

"Yamada's Climbing Silver," he explained to Penelope, informing her of the name of the opening Fei had chosen, as she was *gote* or the player that moved first. "Fujii Sota used that last week during the NHK cup against Watanabe. It didn't work out well…."

"I know, I saw the game. I thought you might enjoy it," said Fei with a smile.

The inspector gave Fei a little bow of thanks, and made the appropriate move in response to her opening.

Fei nodded at her friend. "You know why she is here tonight, right? She wants to pump you for information about the Takahashi case. She thinks he was bumped off."

Penelope rolled her eyes. "I'm just here to say hello. Don't listen to her."

The inspector smiled and polished his glasses with the small cloth he kept in his neat little glasses case.

"That case… yes. That's another reason I've been busy," he said. "We've been collecting statements from all the family and the staff and other people who were there. I was going to ask you to come down to the station and give us yours, would you mind? I believe you were one of the first people to see the body?"

Penelope lowered her head, a little embarrassed.

"Sure, I can do that. How about tomorrow morning?"

"That would be fine," he said.

"She can never resist seeing a fresh corpse," said Fei.

"Not true again," said Penelope, who had actually seen a few in her time with Fei. "By the way, though, did you speak to Haruko? I was wondering where she was during that evening."

"See what I mean," muttered Fei.

The inspector ignored her.

"Ah yes, the Merry Widow. Yes, we spoke to her. She was out having dinner with a friend. Got home about nine-thirty. Didn't see anything. Went to bed. Took a sleeping tablet. Didn't see anything, hear anything... nothing."

"Oh. I see," said Penelope

The inspector made another move and leaned back in his chair.

"Also, never shed a tear. Not one. Odd, I thought."

"Is that so? She didn't like her husband?" asked Penelope.

"No one liked her husband," interjected Fei.

The inspector nodded. "That does seem to be the general consensus about the man, I admit."

"He was a difficult person by all accounts. I can't say I liked him either," said Penelope. "But he *did* remarry after his first wife Sachiko died. I always wondered why, actually. Maybe he was in love... Haruko is a lot younger than him."

Fei snorted. "He was an *iemoto* in a tea school. Wives are important to those guys. It's seen as weird if you don't have one. They do a lot of the work; you know that. And, of course, she married him for his money. Or the money she thought he had. Whatever, it was not some big romance."

Penelope nodded. What Fei said was true. In the ultra-conservative world of tea, a wife was an asset and seen as necessary in the running of the school.

"What about Momoko? And Issei?" she asked.

"They had dinner with Papa. Everything was fine; I thought that was weird for a start. They watched a movie in the library after dinner. Went to bed afterward, big day the next day with the *ochakai,* etc. Same story. Didn't see anything, didn't hear anything. Yada yada… Ah, your friend here has opened up her right flank. That's what Fujii did last Sunday. It didn't work out well for him, like I said."

"I'm not Fujii Sota," Fei said dryly.

Penelope helped herself to the plate of sesame snacks and noticed Auntie Chen was ensconced in front of the TV with her knitting. Her huge Siamese cat Bei Bei was sitting on its cushion next to her, eyeing the line of yarn as it slowly wiggled towards her fingers from its basket on the floor.

"Did anyone see them in the library?" Penelope asked.

Fei looked up. "See what I mean? Very suspicious…" she smiled.

"Yes, as a matter of fact. The maid. She confirmed they were watching a film."

"Oh. OK. I see. Anyway, more to the point. Did you find out what the big secret was with the *ochakai?* Half of Kamakura is dying to know that. Me too. So…" Penelope gave him her most winning smile.

"Penny-*sensei*, you are going to cost me my pension," the inspector smiled. He picked up a *shogi* piece between his long index and middle fingers and slapped it loudly onto the large *keyaki* wood board in the traditional manner.

"Isn't it going to be common knowledge soon? I don't think Momoko has any reason to keep it a secret..." said Fei.

The inspector agreed.

"I suppose that's true. Issei said he didn't understand why the father wanted to have an *ochakai* to announce it in the first place. He said he should have just sold the thing and been done with it. Just keeping it in the bank wasn't going to do anything, he said. But he said the father was obsessed with it and wanted to make a big deal of it. Very great prestige for the school and all that. So that was the purpose of the *ochakai*, to show it off."

Penny leaned forward, intrigued.

"Sorry, I don't follow you. To show what off?"

Fei looked up and smiled.

"Papa had a new tea bowl," she said.

"A tea bowl? All this was about a tea bowl?"

"Apparently," said the Inspector. "But it was not just any tea bowl, but you would know more about this than me, Penny-*sensei*."

"More about what? A tea bowl?" she asked.

"Sure. I don't know much about tea, as you know. So what would a tea bowl made by Sen no Rikyu be worth? A lot?" he asked.

Penelope felt the blood drain from her face, and her mouth fell open.

Both Fei and the inspector stared at her, obviously amused.

"He had a bowl by... *Rikyu*?" she whispered.

"Yes. It was recently discovered in some old building he had knocked down on the estate."

Penelope sat back in her seat, stunned.

"Well, now I understand....."

"So it's a big deal?" asked Fei.

"Yes, it's a very big deal. I think there are only a very few of them, and they are in museums as far as I know. To own one yourself... that's unbelievable," she said.

"So he would have wanted to show it off?" said the inspector.

Penelope nodded. "Knowing him? Definitely. It's priceless. Most people have never seen such a thing."

"How much would something like that go for? You know, at auction?"

Penelope shook her head and shrugged.

"As far as I know, something like that has never been auctioned. It would be millions, though."

"Millions of yen?" asked Fei.

Penelope nodded.

"Millions and millions..." she said.

The inspector gave a low whistle.

"It could be any price. It would be worth whatever someone is willing to pay for it. And there are a lot of people in the tea world that would give their left leg for something like that," she said. "Did the family know about it?"

"Yes, he told them about a week before he died. But he swore them to secrecy," he said. "You said millions? Tens of millions? Hundreds?"

'Yes. It could be," said Penelope.

The inspector and Fei exchanged glances, and Penelope remembered that she was talking to a police officer and not just a friend.

"Sounds like motive to me," said the inspector.

"Maybe, but remember he died in a locked room and all the family, who are the only ones who benefit, have an alibi," said Fei.

The inspector nodded, but he was clearly considering the options.

"Oh, don't tell me you are going to the dark side," said Fei, as she slapped down her move with a precise sounding click. "He poisoned himself. That's clear."

The inspector shrugged and studied the board.

"With cyanide," Penelope said.

"That's right," said Fei.

"Doesn't that strike you as odd?"

"No, why? You can buy that stuff on Amazon," said Fei.

And did he? It seems weird to me that a seventy-year-old tea teacher would know anything about that sort of thing. Wouldn't he have looked it up on the internet? You know... how to use it? Dosage etc.? Wouldn't that be on his computer at home?"

The inspector looked at her.

"You know, Penny-*sensei*, there are times I would like to hire you," he said with a warm smile. "That's an interesting thought...."

"Have you considered he might have just gone to the library and done his research there? You remember those places, don't you, Penny?" said Fei.

"That's possible," said Penelope. "If I wanted to cover my tracks, I would do my research online at the library."

Fei shook her head. "I give up," she said with a smile. "Check, by the way," she said to the inspector, who looked down at the board in surprise.

"Hmmm… Fujii Sota never thought of that," he said in disbelief.

Fei smiled. "I told you, I'm not Fujii Sota. I'm better…"

Penelope kept her thoughts to herself. It was time she went and paid a visit to Momoko, she thought.

Chapter 7

A Daughter of Tea

A few days later, in the company of Fujimoto-san, who was like a second mother to Momoko, Penelope was invited up to the Takahashi estate for morning tea, ostensibly to see how she was getting on after the funeral.

It was still very warm for September, but Penelope felt she was beginning to see the first signs of autumn in the air. The pampas grass was swaying by the side of the road, and the intense sound of the cicadas seemed noticeably less.

The bus drew up once more outside the estate, and the two ladies, this time in more comfortable Western clothes, made their way up the driveway.

Momoko met them at the door, dressed in an ankle-length orange sun dress with her luxurious black hair trailing down her bare back.

"It's just us, I'm afraid," she apologized. "Haruko is still in bed, she never gets up till about noon. Issei didn't come home last night at all, as usual. So... I asked Eriko to make some tea. Come in and have a seat," she said, escorting them into the library, where the big doors to the terrace stood open to admit the breeze.

"We are sorry to put you out, dear. We just wanted to see how you were getting on after... well, you know... everything," said Fujimoto-san.

Momoko sat on the sofa opposite them, looked at the floor for a moment, and then clasped her pretty hands together.

"Oh, I'm fine. Don't worry about me. To tell the truth, it's been much more peaceful the last few days, especially since all the visitors stopped coming to pay their respects. Is it always like this after funerals? I don't even remember much about Mama's... I was about thirteen at the time. Just that there were lots of people. Papa sent me back to school almost immediately," she said.

Momoko had been educated at a private girls' school in Tokyo, and as the school was a fair distance away from Kamakura, she had usually stayed during the week with one of her aunts who lived in Setagaya ward, one of the capital's more affluent areas.

Eriko then arrived with the tea and some cakes on a large silver platter, leaving them to talk.

"Here, I'll do that," said Fujimoto-san, offering to pour the tea. "My word, this thing weighs a ton," she remarked as she hefted the heavy silver teapot.

"It was my grandmother's. They picked it up when they were in France. It doesn't get much use, but I've always liked it. You know, it's history...."

"I remember you were a history major once, weren't you?" said Penelope.

"Yes, I was. It seems ages ago now. I majored in Japanese history. Well, in this family, what else would you do...."

Penelope smiled.

Momoko had been a student at Hassei University, where Penelope had taught, and she knew the girl's professor, who had spoken highly of her.

"I bumped into Professor Okubo the other day while shopping," Penelope said, mentioning Momoko's old tutor.

"Oh, I haven't seen him for ages. How is he?"

"Oh, very well. He's retired now, like me, of course."

"He helped me when I wrote my thesis. He was very nice, I always thought."

"What was the thesis on again?"

Momoko laughed. "The tea ceremony, of course. Mainly Rikyu," she said.

The three women were silent for a moment and sipped their tea before Penelope broke in on their reveries.

"Momoko san, speaking of Rikyu… I heard about the tea bowl."

Fujimoto-san, to whom she had not confided the news from the inspector, gave Penelope a confused look.

Momoko just nodded. "Yes. He told us about it the week before he died after the authentication came back from Osaka. He made us all swear not to say a word. I think he wanted to make a big show at the *ochakai*. It was supposed to be a surprise for everyone."

"Well, it was certainly a surprise for me, I can tell you that," Penelope said, finishing her tea and placing the fine bone china cup on the highly polished table between them.

"I'm sorry, what are we talking about?" said Fujimoto-san.

Momoko turned to her and smiled. "Do you remember that old tea house we had pulled down a few months ago?"

"Oh, that old thing. Yes, why?"

"Well, apparently, they found an old metal box hidden in one of the walls. One of our ancestors hid it there, probably at least two hundred or more years ago during the Edo Period. To tell the truth, I didn't know the building was so old. Anyway, they found a tea bowl in the box and a letter explaining what it was," Momoko said.

"So, what was it?"

Momoko paused and said quietly, "It was a tea bowl made by Sen no Rikyu."

Fujimoto-san went pale, and her cup clattered on its saucer.

"You're joking," she said,

"I'm not," said Momoko.

"And you had it authenticated?"

Momoko nodded. "Yes. Papa kept it a secret from us, of course, but he sent it to Professor Tanaka at Osaka University. He specializes in that kind of stuff. It's the real thing and matches some of the other Rikyu bowls in the museum. The professor said it is one of the best of the few that exist. I read the report myself. That and the letter with it confirm it."

"You're sure about this?" said Fujimoto-san.

"Yes. As sure as we can be anyway. It's the real thing. One of our ancestors received the bowl from his teacher, one of Rikyu's main disciples in Sakai."

Sakai, a small town south of Osaka, had been a major center for the tea ceremony after Rikyu had been forced to commit suicide for offending Toyotomi Hideyoshi, the *kampaku* and the country's top military leader in the sixteenth century.

"My God," said Fujimoto-san. "Have you seen it? Is it here?" she asked.

Momoko shook her head. "Papa insisted on keeping it in the bank with the rest of the family treasures."

Fujimoto-san lowered her head sadly.

"I would love to see it one day..." she said in an awed voice.

"Of course, I will get it out for you to see. Do you want to see a photograph?" she asked, picking up her phone.

Momoko scrolled through some photos and passed her phone to Penelope, who held it so that Fujimoto-san could see.

The photographs showed a large black tea bowl with a rough shiny glaze, which looked like something they would probably use for a thick tea ceremony. There were several photographs from different angles of the bowl sitting on the same table they were now at. Penelope often marveled that ancient tea bowls could look like new ones, as there had been very little change over the centuries in the style used for the tea ceremony. She often thought that if Rikyu himself could time travel into a modern tea ceremony he would hardly have noticed anything different.

All the same, there was something about the photographs that showed the very simple, rustic character of the bowl, which would have been exactly what she would have expected from the master himself.

"It's beautiful," said Penelope. "I didn't know what to expect. But it looks... perfect."

"It is," agreed Fujimoto-san. "And you held it, Momoko-san?"

Momoko nodded.

"Papa didn't want me to, but I did. I couldn't help myself. To hold a bowl made by the founder of the tea ceremony five hundred years ago…. Something he held. I just had to touch it, even just once," Momoko said in a dreamy voice.

"How many others are there?" said Penelope.

"Three or four, I think," said Momoko. "This one is the only one in private hands, though. The rest are in museums."

The women marveled at the photographs.

"So, what are you going to do with it?" Penelope asked. "Are you going to put it in a museum?"

Momoko looked surprised.

"Oh no, we will keep it here. That's my plan. It must never be sold. Never. It must stay here, in the family. We should use it occasionally too. That's what Rikyu would have wanted…" she said firmly.

Penelope nodded and thought that she was probably right. Rikyu was a famously simple and practical man who had no time for shows of wealth.

"It's just so sad Papa never got the chance to show anyone what he had found," she said. "He was awfully proud of it, as you can imagine."

"Yes, it's such a shame. You were here that night when he… passed away, weren't you?" asked Penelope.

Momoko gave her a surprised look.

"Yes, Issei and I were both here. We watched a movie after dinner. Something on Netflix, I forget what. Some American thing. And then we went to bed. It was a rare treat to spend an evening with my brother, as you can imagine!" she rolled her eyes. "I guess he was only here because Papa wanted his help in the morning with the *ochakai*," she said.

"And Haruko was out? Didn't she see your father when she got home?"

Momoko shook her head. "No. They have separate rooms, you know. Always have had. She came home and went straight up to her room, I think. Eriko saw her before she went to bed. I didn't, though. She's always out these days."

"Did she say where she had been?"

"No. She never does, and I don't ask."

Fujimoto-san left them for a moment, and they were alone for a few minutes.

"I'm sorry, Momoko-san. As you can imagine, the police and Fei told me a few things."

"Oh, don't worry about it. It will all be public knowledge soon enough. People had already been asking why he wanted an *ochakai* in the first place. We have to tell them something..." she said calmly.

"They said your father left a message?" asked Penelope

Momoko looked sadly at the floor and nodded.

"Yes, very short. Something about causing trouble. I had no idea what that was all about. He just left it on his desk."

"Wasn't it an email?"

"Yes, but he never sent it. Just left a copy on his desk."

"I was wondering about that. A lot of older people don't know how to use computers. I'm a bit like that too...."

Momoko nodded. "Oh yes, he was the same. His secretary Shimazaki-san did all that sort of thing for him. He sent the odd email, but I don't think he knew anything else much about the internet or anything. He still had one of those folding phones that no one uses anymore too."

Fujimoto-san rejoined them, and they talked about other matters for a few minutes.

"Are they your mother's books, Momoko?" asked Penelope, pointing to a row of books above the television.

Momoko turned and looked.

"Oh yes, those are some of the books she had when she was in university, I think," she said.

Penelope stood and wandered over to the shelves. There was a row of books, all dramas by famous names like Chekov, Ionescu, Shakespeare, and others. One volume of Tom Stoppard's collected plays lay on top of the others..

"Sorry, I just noticed these because they were all in English. Was she a drama student?"

"Yes, I think she was. She studied in Hokkaido. That was where her family was from," said Momoko. "She told me she had been in some high school and university plays. That was as far as it went, though."

"How did she meet your father?" asked Penelope.

"I think they met when Papa went skiing there once. They fell in love straight away, she always told me. They got married just a year later, which was a bit of a rush in the tea world, as you can imagine. Issei was born shortly afterward. A little bit of a scandal at the time that..." she smiled.

Momoko's mother, Sachiko, had died about ten years previously. She had come from a well-known tea family in Kyoto but had grown up in Hokkaido, where her parents had moved to start a small business. Penelope and Fujimoto-san, particularly the latter, had known her quite well when she was alive. She was a beautiful woman with a kind and generous nature, and Momoko looked a lot like her in many ways. In those days, the old *iemoto* had been of a much more amiable temperament, but that had changed markedly after her death and got even worse after he had married Haruko, a marriage most people believed was an arranged one and something that he had been forced to do because of the demands of his position.

Just as they were about to leave, the *iemoto's* widow Haruko walked into the library, dressed in a long blue dress with a floral print that looked like something from a shop in a British high street.

"Hello, I heard your voices. How are you both?" she said, sitting on the arm of the sofa. Haruko was perhaps about forty years old, but looked not much older than Momoko. She had smartly cut shoulder-length black hair, a slender figure, and a way of speaking and dressing that exuded refined elegance.

Fujimoto-san and Penelope were surprised to see her and even more so that she was deigning to speak to them both.

"Would you like some tea or coffee, Haruko-san?" asked Momoko.

"I just asked Eriko to bring me some coffee, thanks," she replied. "I told her to bring it in here."

They asked how she was getting along after the death, but like Momoko, she seemed remarkably composed. Penelope presumed that many of the rumors about their somewhat distant marriage were probably well founded.

"Yes, it's been an awful business. And a complete shock. No one was prepared for this. We don't have a clue what the finances are like either, we still have to sit down with the accountants and figure everything out. I don't even know if we have enough money to go shopping anymore. And then there have been thousands of people trooping through the house, people I have never seen before. All I really want is a bit of peace. Oh, I'm sorry, I wasn't referring to both of you, you know... You're old friends...."

Penelope wondered if that were true but didn't say anything.

"Yes, it must have been an awful shock," said Penelope. "You were out that night, is that right? The night your husband...er ...?"

Haruko nodded calmly. "Yes, I was out having dinner with a friend in Shibuya. I got home about nine or so and went to bed. I had no idea what was happening."

"Did he often go to the tea house at night?"

Haruko shrugged and looked at Momoko for confirmation.

"He might have done. I really don't know. We had fairly separate lives... If he had been in there that night, I would have assumed he was just preparing for the *ochakai*... not... what happened...."

Momoko agreed. "Yes, Issei and I had no idea he was in there. We just came in here after dinner. The last I saw of him was in the dining room."

Penelope looked at Haruko. "So, did you see the light on in the tea house when you came home?" she asked, realizing she was somewhat pushing the boundaries of their friendship.

Haruko shrugged again. "Not that I remember. As I said, I just hit the sack. I was tired after getting back from Shibuya. I think I fell asleep watching the television in bed."

"Yes, you probably get the Shonan-Shinjuku line from there, don't you?" said Penelope

"Yes, and then I got a taxi from Kamakura station. It's funny… going to Shibuya is only a fifty-minute trip, but it feels like going to the moon these days whenever I go to Tokyo. I've become a real country bumpkin living down here for so long," Haruko laughed.

Shortly afterward, the two women took their leave, after assuring Momoko they would come back and that she could call them anytime if she needed something. Momoko appeared to be relatively stable and cheerful though, and not suffering unduly.

"It's probably a relief for the poor thing if you ask me. For both of them, actually," said Fujimoto-san after they had said goodbye at the door.

Penelope agreed. "Yes, he certainly wasn't easy, I guess."

She stopped and looked back at the house as they made their way down the driveway.

"What's the matter? Did you forget something?" asked Fujimoto-san.

"Oh, I was just wondering if you could see the main tea house from here as you walked up the drive. And there it is…." Penelope pointed.

Fujimoto-san looked too. "Yes, of course. Why?"

"Oh, I was just wondering. When I was a teenager in London, my Mum and Dad always waited for me when I came home late from somewhere. And I always dreaded getting the third degree whenever I got home late and saw the light on, and I knew they would be waiting for me." Penelope said with a nostalgic smile.

"Oh, my parents were the same. My father was the worst. He was very strict. Whenever I got home late, it was like a police interrogation," she laughed.

"That's right. So I was just thinking, you know, old habits die hard, and if I lived here and I was walking up this driveway at night, I would probably notice whatever lights were on in the house... or in the tea house there?" said Penelope, nodding in the direction of the tea house.

Fujimoto-san gave her a strange look but didn't say anything.

"Except Haruko didn't, did she," said Penelope quietly, "which means he must have died between dinner and 9 pm. Quite early. And the light in the tea room must have been switched off, or she would have seen it, I'm sure..."

"No, I guess she didn't see a light, as you say. Anyway, There's the bus. Let's move!" she said, and they hurried down the driveway and waved at the driver, who looked like he was just about to close the door.

Chapter 8.

The Gardeners

Whatever else Penelope did every day, she devoted at least a part of and often the whole day to writing her books. It was a habit she had begun right at the very beginning of her career after coming to Japan, and it was something she had never ceased to do, no matter what. Writing for her was just a part of her day. It was who she was, and she could not imagine herself not writing. Somewhere in the back of her mind, like most writers, no matter what she was doing, there was always a part of her that was thinking about her latest book.

It was a habit that had made her one of the most prolific academics in Japan and garnered her many awards over the years, not to mention a way of adding to her meager pension. And although her books were mainly academic and connected in some way or other with Japanese literature, quite a few had been on other topics, such as a book on sumo she had written, of which she and Fei were big fans, and a couple on the tea ceremony she had been asked to collaborate on with other Japanese authors.

The pace of her output had slowed since she retired, not because she was tired or busy doing other things, but because she was now savoring her topics to a larger degree, spending much more time planning her book and editing and rewriting the finished product. She had never much liked the editing stage of any book that much, much preferring the actual writing, but now the polishing side of things had taken over in her mind as something worth spending more time on, and she would often find herself spending an entire day sometimes redrafting a single chapter or even just a single page until she was happy with it.

Today she had been free and up writing since the early morning. Over the last few months, her topic had been a book about the early twentieth-century Zen poet Santoka Taneda, about whom very little had been written in English. Santoka had been a prolific poet, having written thousands and thousands of haiku, and also one of the last true 'wandering poet monks", living on alms, walking and writing haiku and drinking sake, the latter probably to the point where it killed him. Penelope found him, for some reason, a particularly romantic, deep subject and found herself sitting for hours looking at his simple, unstyled poetry and marveling at the rawness and depth with which this ragged poet described his feelings and the world around him.

She usually wrote in her study, but sometimes she brought her laptop and sat at the kitchen table, usually with one or more of her cats joining her on the table for company.

Her kitchen was relatively small, as is the norm in old Japanese houses such as hers, but it opened out onto the living area, which in turn opened onto the verandah and the garden, which was her favorite part of the house. Sitting at her dining table in the living room, she could survey the many vegetables that she and Fei had planted, and it was these that usually drew her outside every day to tend to them, whether they needed it or not, just for the pleasure of being outside and watching things grow. This little bit of extra land she had been able to get was one of the main reasons she had been attracted to buying this house in the first place after it had been suggested to her one day by Fei, who lived just next door and had known the previous owners, an old couple who were avid gardeners themselves.

This afternoon she had finished her writing for the day and had wandered down the road to the small shop she often visited to pick up some fish she needed for dinner. She usually avoided the big supermarkets if possible unless there was something she couldn't find locally, even though they were often quite a bit cheaper. She found shopping locally was more pleasant; she knew all the shopkeepers well, especially at the little supermarket run by the elderly Mori sisters where she usually shopped, and she often spent a little time there catching up on the local gossip with them or with old Enamoto san, from whom she loyally bought all her fish.

This afternoon she stopped at both places, and the Mori sisters, Emi and Kimi, had sat her down and given her some cold tea before she left.

"I've never seen such a dreadful summer," Kimi complained as she rearranged some packets of bonito flakes on the shelves. "I mean, this heat, it just seems never-ending."

Penelope agreed. The summers did seem to be getting hotter and longer, and every year particularly in August, the reports of disasters with flooding and mudslides and the like, particularly in Kyushu and the western regions of the country dominated the news broadcasts.

After buying a few simple provisions for dinner, which this time of year she would usually supplement with some summer vegetables from her garden, and also catching up on the latest news about someone's divorce and someone else's daughter being accepted into such and such a university, she went back home to find Fei sitting in her usual chair in the living room with her pipe and her newspaper. On Saturdays or Sundays, Fei usually joined her for a meal, either lunch or dinner or both, and though neither would ever say so, both women enjoyed being in the other's company and working in the vegetable garden together in the afternoons when it was not too hot. Sometimes she would even find Fei there in the early summer mornings, watering the plants before she went to work.

A lot of their relationship operated in these unspoken ways, with one helping the other without being asked, or buying something one of them needed and leaving it on the table. It was just how they were together and how it had always been between them, like they were an old married couple or twin sisters who could finish each other's sentences.

"I hear you and Fujimoto-san were up at the Takahashi's the other day?" she asked without looking up from her paper as Penelope dumped her shopping on the table.

"Yes, it was very interesting," said Penelope, as she went to the refrigerator to get some cold barley tea for them both, one of the staple drinks in Japan in the summer months.

The doors to the garden wear open, and Fei had lit a couple of mosquito coils which she had placed on the little wooden verandah, as the insects were a problem at this time of year, especially after it rained.

"So, did the butler do it? Oh, that's right, they don't have a butler. Don't you think it's surprising they don't have a butler? I'm sure Papa would have loved to have an extra body to scream at all day…" said Fei.

"They couldn't afford one, from what I heard. They were going broke, according to Momoko," said Penelope, sitting in the other comfortable wicker chair opposite her friend and putting her feet up on the little glass coffee table. "What does it say in the newspaper?"

Penelope hardly ever turned on the television or read the newspaper, so half the time she had no idea what was happening and relied on Fei, who was a voracious reader of newspapers and news in general.

"Nothing much, except it should rain tomorrow morning, so that might save you watering," she said. "Anyway, they won't be going broke with that bowl, will they? You said it was worth a bomb."

Penelope sighed. "Well, it may be worth a bomb, but according to Momoko, they will never sell it."

Fei looked up with an amused look on her face. "Why not? They'd rather go broke?"

"It appears so."

"They must be bonkers. By the way, that's my new word for the day. "bonkers," Fei grinned. "Like, 'they must be bleedin' bonkers, roight?'"

"Yes, well, some people might say that," said Penelope with a smile.

Fei was a great devotee of English slang words, much to Penelope's amusement. They had once been to the Camden Markets in London, and Fei had been delighted to come back with a swag of new slang that she had taken great pleasure developing ever since. Her English conversation was thus peppered with words like 'dosh', 'flog', 'slag', 'frog and toad', 'dog and bone', 'shag,' and her perennial favorite 'innit'. Hearing a respected Japanese doctor such as her describing some situation she had read about in the newspaper along the lines of 'that's a real bit of a dog's breakfast, innit?', was one of the joys of having Fei around at any time.

"I'm surprised bloody Papa didn't want to flog it. He was a money-mad old hound from all accounts."

"Yes, that crossed my mind too. But once you have 'flogged it' as you so colorfully put it, then you don't have it. And then you can't show it off…" she said. "And he was definitely a show-off, as you are well aware, I'm sure."

"True," Fei said. "He was that, wasn't he." Fei finished her tea in a few gulps and lit her pipe, and they both watched the smoke curling around the mosquito coils and floating out over the garden with its green tangle of eggplants and tomatoes and about thirty other things they were growing in every available corner.

"By the way, here is something I heard that will warm the cockles of your heart," remarked Fei, "What is a 'cockle' anyway, I wonder. It's not a medical term I am familiar with…."

"And what might that be?" asked Penelope.

"Haruko. Guess what Haruko was before she got married to his highness?"

"I can't. Shock me."

"She was an industrial chemist," said Fei, arching her eyebrow.

"You're kidding."

"I kid thee not. She worked for some big pharmaceutical company in Osaka."

"Well, that's interesting…." said Penelope.

"I'm waiting for you to say, 'So she knows all about poisons.'"

"Well, I was just about to say that, how did you know?"

"Because I'm psychic," said Fei, folding her newspaper.

"So she was not involved in the tea world?" asked Penelope

"Nope. That was her family. Her father and mother actually, they own this old shop in Kyoto that's been in the family for hundreds of years. They make sweets for the tea ceremony, mainly. You've probably been to it, it's pretty well-known."

Penelope racked her brains.

"It's not the Obayashi place, is it?"

Fei nodded.

"The very one."

Penelope slapped her leg.

"You're right, I have been to it. That's where Fujimoto-san gets all her sweets, I think."

"Well, that's Haruko's family. They have a long connection with the Takahashi family, I hear."

"Doesn't surprise me, that shop is very well known in the tea world."

Penelope began to say something, and then she stopped.

"That's strange," she said.

"What?" asked Fei.

"There were no sweets in the room."

"What room?"

"The room he died in."

Fei went to the refrigerator and got them some more tea.

"Well, it was the middle of the night. Maybe he couldn't be bothered?"

They were silent for a while and contemplated the garden.

"If I were going to have a final bowl of tea, my very last one, I would want a sweet to go with it. Especially if I was an old tea master like him…." she said.

In the tea ceremony, eating a sweet before you drank the tea was the normal, accepted way of doing things. The sweet balanced the bitterness of the tea and was seen as an almost essential part of the ceremony. No one would ever think of hosting a tea gathering or even just a lesson in your house without providing a sweet. This was why there were still many old shops all around the country, not to mention in all of the big department stores, that sold *wagashi* or Japanese sweets, many of which could be used in the tea ceremony, and many of which were specifically made for it.

"I guess so. It doesn't mean he couldn't have done without it, though," said Fei.

"No… I suppose so."

"And anyway… Haruko? You saw her too, up at the house?"

Penelope nodded, "Yes. We mainly talked to Momoko, but she dropped in before we left."

"OK, so where was she on the fateful night?"

"Haruko? She said she was in Shibuya. With a friend," said Penelope.

"Which friend?" asked Fei.

"I don't know. She didn't say."

"I know who it was," said Fei with a mischievous smile.

Penelope gave her a stern look.

"And you know this... from Yamashita san?"

Fei nodded. "You are going to like this. She was out having dinner with another guy."

"Seriously?"

"Yep. Given the state of her marriage, it might look like a good career move."

Penelope laughed.

"So, who was the guy?" she asked.

"That's even more interesting. You know the Inamoto School of Tea?"

"Inamoto... not really. Is that in Ibaraki?" asked Penelope, searching her memory.

"I think so. Not sure," said Fei. "But anyway, she was out dining at some swanky place with the son and heir of old Inamoto *iemoto*. Papa has one leg in the grave, and he inherits the title."

"That's a much smaller school than the Takahashi school, I think."

Fei nodded. "Yes, I googled it. They only started up after the war, I think. Pretty small, but very rich. Papa's wife? She's the Morisaka heiress. Got the majority of the shares in the company."

"Oh! OK, now I remember them. Yes. The beverages company? They make that sake we like; what's it called?"

"*Rissho*."

"That's the one," Penelope recalled. "So she got all that?"

"Yep, she got the works. And sonny boy, I forget his name, but he is the only child. So they might be a small tea school, but they have pots of money. Unlike the Takahashi's. She's a smart girl, that Haruko."

Penelope smiled wryly. "So it would seem...."

Later that afternoon, Penelope cut up the piece of sea bream she had bought earlier, and they had it as *sashimi*, much to the delight of all four cats, who had come running at the scent of it and were also given a little treat.

They then spent an hour in the garden watering all the plants and weeding and picking a few things to go with their dinner, a simple meal of rice and vegetables with a small pudding for dessert. Fei also opened some cold sake, and they sat and drank it together on the verandah after their baths.

"The mosquitoes are not so bad this year," Fei commented as she looked out on the twilight garden.

"No," said Penelope.

Her mind had been on the Takahashi saga all afternoon and also on the various doings of the family. The thought nagged her that something was not right with the story they had all been expected to believe.

"Did Yamashita-san ever investigate the computer angle? You know, look at the *iemoto's* internet history?"

"Ah, that again," said Fei. "Yes, he did. There was nothing on it. The old boy hardly ever touched a computer, he said. Makes sense. My aunt wouldn't even know how to plug one in. They were about the same age."

Penny nodded. "That's probably true. And that's also what bugs me."

"What?"

89

Penny poured them both some more sake. "First, he poisons himself with cyanide. Where did he get that? And wouldn't he check it out first on the internet? You know, as I said before? And yes, I know he could go to the library and do it, but why bother when he has a computer at home? And also, from the sound of it, he didn't even know what Google was."

"True," said Fei. "Maybe Haruko told him all about it," she said with an evil smile.

Penelope laughed. "So, excuse me, darling, I, your aged husband whom everyone dislikes, especially you, would like to know all about cyanide. Could you possibly help me out?"

Fei laughed. "Hey, when you put it like that, I'm sure she couldn't wait to assist. Probably went out and bought it in bulk."

"Right. And then there is the note."

"Ah, the note. I was wondering when you would get to that," said Fei.

"Well, I am at it now."

"Haruko could have written it," suggested Fei, tossing back her sake.

"Yep. She could have. That's my point. Anyone could have written it. But why would a man who almost never touched a computer suddenly sit down, write an email, not send it and print it out? Why wouldn't he just pick up a pen and write it?" said Penny, staring into the gathering darkness.

"Yes, I wondered that too, I must admit," said Fei. "It does seem a bit odd. But people do odd things before they top themselves. It's not the most stable of mental states."

"I dunno, Fei. He was a *chajin*, a real tea master. I don't think he was panicking. Everything about his last moments was orderly and planned. He even laid a fire in the brazier to boil the water. He didn't have to do that. He could have just boiled the kettle. Lots of people make tea that way when they are in a hurry. There was an electric kettle and a plug in the room, I've seen them before."

Fei was silent, as if conceding the point.

"No, he took his time. He did the whole thing properly in a planned way. He didn't skip on the details in his last moments. It was all there."

"Except no sweets," interjected Fei.

"That's right. No sweets…"

Chapter 9

A Scandal

Penelope remembered that her first encounter with anything Japanese was hearing about the death of the author Yukio Mishima when she was in high school. Her English teacher, Alice Symmons, a wiry old woman who was probably the best-read person she had met before or since had given her an article about him one day and urged her students to read Mishima, telling them he was 'important.'

What she had meant by 'important' was "completely different from and possibly much better than Western writers,' and this was something that had intrigued her from the very beginning.

The first thing she noticed when she started reading, particularly his four-novel 'Sea of Fertility' series, is how Mishima would lead you into a story with the focus on the small and often symbolic details and then trust you as his reader to figure them out. And it was this level of indirectness, which is an extremely common trait not just in writing but in Japanese society generally, that appealed to her greatly and led her to begin learning Japanese as a language, simply because she wanted to understand how it was used and also how you could possibly translate some of the things that she was reading in Mishima.

If Penelope had any one defining trait herself, it was a possibly over-exuberant sense of curiosity. This stood her in good stead when she started learning Japanese, which she did at first in secret.

During her last year of high school and her first year at Oxford, she hid her Japanese textbooks and tapes in plain covers marked with completely different titles. Her large Japanese textbook perched quietly on a shelf above her desk with a cover that read 'Chemistry 3.0', whereas the cassettes that went with it sat in their little plastic cases with 'Joni Mitchell Live' written on them.

In her free time, for at least an hour a day and often more, she began to study this absurdly complicated language without telling anyone what she was doing. She had taken French for a while in school, but this was the first time she had learned a language completely on her own - simply because she wanted to do it. There was no reason for it, as she had no real intention of ever going to Japan or taking her involvement to a higher level. Still, the more she studied, the more the language and the country's quiet but beautiful culture called to her and made her feel in some strange way at home and comfortable. She started reading more and more books, not just Mishima, but Tanizaki, Kawabata, and poets like Basho and Buson. She started looking into the ancient classics like the *Tale of Genji* and the *Pillow Book*.

And slowly but inexorably, she knew what she wanted to do.

One day, halfway through her first year, she informed the university that she wanted to major in Japanese language and literature, and at the beginning of her second year, she began to take the available courses in those subjects.

And this was where everything began to change for her. She completely threw herself into her language studies, to such a degree that sometimes she dreamt in the language. And now, suddenly, she met an actual Japanese person for the first time in her life.

She remembered going into her first ever actual language class and seeing her teacher, a small and tranquil woman called Dr. Kobayashi, walk into the room, her long black hair swaying behind her slender form as she walked up to the blackboard.

"*Hajimemashite. Kobayashi to moshimasu...*" the teacher began... Hello, my name is Kobayashi."

"Ladies and gentlemen. Let us begin," she said in English.

And they began.

Some forty-five years later, Penelope opened the door of Fujimoto-san's familiar tea room on her knees and bowed until her hair just grazed the floor. She then rose, entered the room, and went back onto her knees to shut the sliding door with both hands, and then greeted Momoko and her teacher, who were already waiting for her.

Momoko had always been a frequent guest at Fujimoto-san's tea lessons, just as the latter had often visited the Takahashi estate to use their tea houses.

Penelope, who had been studying tea with the old lady for twenty-five years, had known Momoko since she had been in junior high school when she had attended these lessons in her school uniform. She had also been quite well acquainted with Momoko's mother, Sachiko, who was clearly where Momoko got her stunning good looks from.

Her mother had been a noted beauty and a distant relation to a branch of the royal family that had lost its titles and estates after the war. The family still lived in some style, even if they could not afford to do so any longer, and Sachiko had attended one of the best schools and even been to the imperial palace a few times to meet some of her now distant relatives.

Of course, the family had long been connected to the tea world and the Takahashi school in particular, so when the old *iemoto* had suggested a union between his son and heir and their daughter, this had not at all been seen as an inappropriate match, especially considering that the Takahashi's at that time had been relatively well off and were certainly well connected.

Today they had all dressed in *kimono*, and they had all coincidentally decided to wear an autumn leaf pattern on their *kimono* or *obi*, as it was now late September and the weather was definitely beginning to show signs of change. The nights were now cooler, and in the evenings in particular the sound of cicadas singing in the trees was beginning to be replaced by the sound of *suzumushi*, or the autumn crickets, that were so much a part of the season, and also the poetry that was written about it.

"Oh, I'm glad you are here, Penny-*sensei*," said Fujimoto-san, as Penelope sat down in the formal *seiza* position next to Momoko and arranged her little folding fan in front of her.

"Me too," said Momoko with a smile. "It's so lovely to get away from home for a few hours. It's been terrible up there recently."

"Really? What's going on," asked Penelope.

Momoko looked upset.

"Oh, Issei mainly. He's decided to take over the school."

Penelope and Fujimoto-san exchanged glances.

"Oh, I kind of assumed he would do that. He is the heir, isn't he?"

Momoko nodded.

"Yes... and no. Papa originally intended it that way, but he was having doubts, apparently. Especially when Issei told him about... the money," she said.

Penelope raised her eyebrows. "The money?"

"Well..." Momoko began. "I shouldn't tell you this, but I know you will be discreet...."

"Of course," said Fujimoto-san. "Is there a problem with money?"

Momoko nodded her pretty head, and Penelope noticed she was wearing one of her mother's elegant black lacquerware combs.

"You all know Issei likes to play mahjong, I guess. Everybody knows that."

Penelope smiled. "Yes, I think we have all heard that story. He's a bit of a young pirate, like a lot of young men, I suppose," she said.

Momoko agreed and picked up her fan, opening and shutting it in a distracted way.

"Well, what we didn't know until earlier this year, is that he was gambling. And he lost money. A lot of money...."

Although it was extremely common, gambling on games like mahjong was illegal, not that the police ever really did anything about it. There were thousands of mahjong parlors throughout the country where this kind of 'grey area' crime was carried on daily.

"I'm sorry to hear that," said Fujimoto-san. "How much is a lot, though?"

Momoko looked at the floor miserably.

'I'm not sure. Maybe ten or twenty million yen...."

Fujimoto-san and Penelope exchanged another worried look.

"Wow," said Penelope. "That's a lot."

Momoko nodded. "That's not the end of the story, though."

"It isn't?" said Fujimoto-san incredulously.

"No," said Momoko. "Originally, the money he lost was his inheritance from our grandfather, my mother's father, who left money to Issei and me in his will. He never really liked Papa that much and wanted to ensure we were looked after, especially when Mama died. Anyway... Issei seems to have spent all his money. There was the car, you know about that, I'm sure, and then he blew a pile of money in Ginza and Kabukicho on hostess bars. And then there was the gambling... and so it's all gone...."

They were all silent for a moment, and then Momoko continued.

"But after it was all gone... he continued to gamble. And he borrowed money to do it."

"Oh my God," said Penelope. "From his friends?"

"Partly, but a lot of it was from... well, you can guess. Those people often are connected to the gambling business…" she said, placing her fan on the floor and then sitting up straight and looking at them.

There was only one group of people to whom she could be referring, and Fujimoto-san and Penelope were both well aware of who it was.

Issei had been borrowing money from gangsters, which meant the Japanese *yakuza*.

For the heir to the house of Takahashi, the son of a respected Grandmaster of the Tea ceremony, it was hard to imagine a greater scandal than this. Even the faintest breath of a connection to a criminal gang would be enough to ruin anybody in the classical Japanese arts, let alone someone in the ultra-conservative world of the tea ceremony. The school and the grandmasters that had overseen it down through the centuries had not only been connected with many influential people past and present but had been on close terms with the Japanese royal family for over a century.

Neither Fujimoto-san nor Penelope knew what to say.

"In the end, he had to tell Papa and beg for his help. Otherwise, he said, they were going to kill him," she said, her voice shaking slightly.

"What did your father do?" asked Fujimoto-san.

Momoko shrugged.

"He paid, of course. What else could we do? If it ever got out…" she looked at them both. "Please… don't tell anyone, I beg you. It's just been so hard with no one to talk to about this… and with everything recently…" she gave a profound sigh and looked away.

"You don't have to worry, Momoko. No one will hear of this from us," said Fujimoto-san, who got up from her place and sat next to the girl with her arm around her shoulders.

Momoko raised her tear-stained face and nodded gratefully to them both.

'I don't know. It's just the shamefulness of it all. I didn't realize how much it would affect me. But it did…."

"I understand," said Penelope consolingly. "But hopefully, he has learned his lesson now. And if he is going to become *iemoto*… he has a lot of motivation to change."

Momoko sighed.

"I'm not so sure about that. And neither was Papa, actually. I've never seen him so angry and so sad. I think it took a toll on his mind. Maybe it was even the reason he…." she left the sentence unfinished and held her fan tightly in her fist.

"He had a conversation with me privately one day, not long before he…died. Did you know our school has a precedent for the *iemoto* to be a woman?"

Penelope opened her eyes wide, as did Fujimoto-san.

It was highly unusual in Japanese society, of the past at least, for a woman to succeed a male in an important position such as the head of a traditional tea school. Penelope and many others had always thought this very incongruous indeed though, as in the tea world, 99% of all students were women. Even with that being the case, all the hierarchy of the schools were men. That was just the way things were.

However, it was not without precedent for a woman to take charge in certain situations, especially in the case of the lack of a male heir.

Even in the royal family, which since the Meiji constitution had been promulgated in the 1870s which had set out in law for the first time that the emperor had to be male, there had been eight former female emperors, two of whom had ascended the throne a second time. One of these had even passed on the throne to her daughter.

So even though it was pretty well unheard of in the tea world for this to happen, there was no actual law against it. It was simply precedent and nothing else. For a woman in the twenty-first century to take control of a significant tea organization like the Takahashi school could even be seen as a step in the right direction.

Nevertheless, there were bound to be many problems with it in practice, not the least being that there was an existing male heir.

"A woman *iemoto*? I didn't know about that," said Penelope.

Momoko nodded. "In the nineteenth century in our school, there were two. One was the wife of one of our ancestors who died young without any children, and the other time it was because the male heir died. She ran the school for nearly fifteen years before passing the title to her child, who was a male. So it has happened. Papa was aware of this, and he spoke to me about it a few times actually," she said quietly.

"Of course, I know it's impossible. Especially with Issei. And now he claims he wants to take over the title and run the school himself. Haruko is right behind him, of course. I don't think she wants to be seen as in the way or anything," she added.

The three women were silent as they took in what Momoko was implying, and Penelope and Fujimoto-san felt genuinely sorry for the poor girl. Given Issei's character, there was no question that she would have made a much better choice for taking over the school than her brother. But without a clear indication from her father that proved this was his will, it would be next to impossible if there was an existing male heir that wanted the job.

Usually, in the tea world, an heir to the title was formally announced some years before the retirement of an *iemoto*, however, this had not yet taken place with the Takahashi school, and maybe it was true that the reason for the delay was that the old man had been considering his options regarding Issei.

"So when is all this going to take place?" said Fujimoto-san. She gestured to Penelope to take her place in front of the kettle and make some tea for them all, which Penelope duly did.

Momoko sat up and gave a brave smile. "I don't know. As soon as possible, I think. I think they will start writing to people soon and probably organize a big *ochakai* to mark the occasion. It's just that I'm worried. Issei and Haruko have control of the school and any money that now remains. I'm concerned about what they are going to do with it. And I'm worried if there will be anything left when they have finished."

Penelope handed them some sweets to eat before giving them the tea.

"Well, it sounds like they want to keep everything going. Maybe having a new young *iemoto* will be good for a change," said Fujimoto-san.

"Maybe," said Momoko unenthusiastically.

The tea lesson ended in the usual way. Momoko made tea next, and Penelope and Fujimoto-san steered the conversation as deliberately as possible away from the subject of Momoko's family until the young woman had brightened up and was smiling again when she and Penelope parted ways outside the house. Momoko, meanwhile, promised to come again the following week and let them know what was happening.

Penelope headed back towards her home, just around the corner from Fujimoto-san's house. Once there, she quickly took off her *kimono*, which she found quite uncomfortable outside when the weather was still humid like today, and made herself some lunch.

There was something that Momoko had said that was nagging at her, so she decided to see if she could find out some more information.

She went into her study and, opening up her computer, looked up the Takahashi school of tea on the internet. There were dozens of pages relating to it, but eventually, she could find what she wanted, a list of the previous *iemoto* since the School's founding in the 1670s.

Scrolling through the list, sure enough, she found the name of two women who had been *iemoto* at one time or another during the School's long history, just as Momoko had said.

What made her wonder, though, was why Momoko had brought this subject up in the first place. Had her father really been hatching a plan to replace his errant son with his daughter? Although it was possible, having known the old man well as she did, it didn't sound like something he would contemplate unless he were under extreme duress. He was one of the most conservative and therefore probably misogynistic Japanese men she had ever known.

Penelope quietly added it to the growing number of things about this case that didn't make sense and decided to bring the matter up with the chief inspector at the next opportunity.

The longer she thought about all of this, the more she became convinced that the old man had not committed suicide.

So that left only one alternative, and it was an alternative that no one seemed to be considering except her.

Chapter 10

The Great Buddha of Kamakura

The day that Penelope had been quietly dreading for weeks had finally arrived.

Auntie Chen, Fei's aunt, had been preparing for her relative's visit to Japan for months, and an exact itinerary had been handed to Fei some weeks previously, which reduced her options regarding escaping her tour guide duties to precisely zero. As a result, she had roped Penelope into the expedition as a support act, and thus she also had been made to set aside the next few days to show Auntie Chen's elderly cousin and her daughter the delights of their little town.

Fortunately, Kamakura was one of the most popular tourist destinations near the capital, and there were many things to see. There were way too many that could be covered in just two days, but from the 'schedule' they had been given, Auntie Chen seemed determined to make an attempt.

On the first day of their excursion, Fei arrived early at Penelope's house in time to catch her with her morning coffee. She had been up early getting some work done for an upcoming deadline, but she was now breakfasted and ready to go. Auntie Chen, she knew, would brook no sign of lateness, and she was not about to stir the dragon any more than necessary.

Fei sat down in her usual chair with a sigh of frustration and waved the schedule in the air.

"If you want to make this work, you'd need to be an Olympic sprinter. There is no way you can see six different temples in different parts of the town in one afternoon. It's ridiculous," she exclaimed.

Penelope sighed too. "Yes, it did seem a bit crazy when I saw that," she agreed. "Maybe we can get her to give up on the last two. Unless she wants to walk around them in the dark…."

Fei leaned forward in her chair and put the palms of her hands together.

"You know she wants to take them to a Chinese restaurant for lunch," she opined.

"Yes, I saw that. It looks like a good choice to me, I've been to the Golden Rose before. The food is pretty good there."

The Golden Rose was a Chinese restaurant near the station and not far from the Great Buddha, which was their destination this morning.

Fei snorted in disbelief. "These people live in Shanghai, and it's the old girl's first time in Japan. Why would you want to take Chinese people who live in Shanghai to a Chinese restaurant?"

"I see your point. But you know your aunt and Japanese food. She probably thinks they will both be dead the next morning if they ate that," replied Penelope, sipping her coffee and watching Alphonse, who was eyeing a little bird that had just alighted on the top of the passionfruit vine outside.

Fei shook her head in disbelief.

"Do you want some coffee?" asked Penelope.

"No thanks, I had mine hours ago when she hauled me out of bed to 'get ready'.

Penelope smiled. This was yet another moment she was always secretly glad she lived alone, but this was probably not the best moment to confess this to her friend.

"So, I suppose we had better get going then? We are still meeting at 10 am?"

Fei nodded.

"10 am at Kamakura station. Auntie has told them they will be taken around by a famous professor of Japanese history. So, they are looking forward to meeting you a lot, I hear."

"What? She knows I'm not a history professor. Why did she tell them that?" said Penelope in a surprised voice.

"Today you are. Don't you dare tell them otherwise, either. Well, you can tell Ling, she is quite nice. I don't know how she puts up with her mother, to tell the truth."

"OK." Penelope sighed. She had an inkling that today was going to be a very long day.

Penelope hurriedly drank her coffee and got ready, and at 10 am on the dot, Fei, Penelope and Auntie Chen finally had a noisy meeting with Mrs. Lu and her daughter Ling at the main Kamakura station.

The first thing Penelope thought as she stood by watching the two women embrace each other repeatedly was that the relationship Mrs. Lu enjoyed with her daughter looked like a carbon copy of Fei and her aunt.

Ling, the daughter, was a pleasant woman in her early fifties who, like Fei, was a doctor. Unlike Fei though, she preferred to help the living rather than the dead, and worked in the emergency ward at one of the biggest hospitals in Shanghai. She had shoulder-length greying hair and large glasses that Penelope thought made her look somewhat like a friendly owl.

Her mother, Mrs. Lu, who spoke only Chinese, was a cousin of Auntie Chen, and the two had not met for many years. This resulted in a tumultuous reunion, and there were a lot of tears and screams of joy before the two elderly women could be forced to continue their reunion somewhere other than the main concourse of Kamakura station during the end of the morning rush hour.

Penelope eventually led the way, and they managed to move in the general direction of where they needed to go.

Ling came up beside her as they walked.

"My mother tells me you are a professor of Japanese history? So, I was expecting a Japanese person today. Are you from America?" she asked as they made their way to the platform of the Enoden line for the short trip to the Great Buddha.

Penelope took her arm.

"I have to tell you a secret. I'm British. And I was a professor of Japanese literature. Not history. I probably know as much as you," she confessed.

"Oh," said Ling. "Well, don't worry. My mother tells all her friends I am Chief Surgeon. That would come as a big surprise to my boss, who is Chief Surgeon. But I am not allowed to say otherwise," she laughed.

"Well, you keep my secret, and I'll keep yours," said Penelope. "Where did you learn to speak such good English?"

"Boston. I was an intern there for five years."

"You went to Harvard?"

"Yep. I was not allowed to go anywhere else," said Ling.

"I guess that makes sense," said Penelope, watching in amusement as Fei tried to explain the ticket machine to her aunt, who was telling her niece in no uncertain terms that the machine had mysteriously 'changed' since her last visit, and the price had gone up, which of course, it hadn't. At least not in the last ten years.

Finally, after a few stops on the pleasantly old-fashioned Enoden line, they arrived at their station and made their way in single file up the narrow little footpath towards Kotoko-in, the temple which housed the Great Buddha.

Most of the streets in Kamakura were very narrow like this, and so a nightmare for drivers of anything larger than a small car. The footpaths like the one they were on now were also very narrow, most of the time just wide enough for a single person with the cars passing perilously close to you while you walked. The city had been left mercifully unmodernized in most respects, but it did result in severe traffic jams, especially when the tour buses were involved. These jams were often so bad that even a bicycle couldn't pass between the vehicles, and it could take hours to go just a few kilometers, much to the fury of the local residents who maybe just wanted to go to the supermarket on the other side of town.

The Great Buddha of Kamakura, as it was called, had been a tourist destination for centuries and was one of the oldest and largest Buddhist statues in the country, so it was a natural starting point for anyone who wanted a tour of the city, as well as being very easy to get to from the city center.

The statue was always an inspiring sight, and Penelope knew a couple of stories about it which she could relate via Ling, who translated them into Shanghainese, the local dialect her mother and Auntie Chen spoke. Both ladies, according to Fei, eschewed the use of Mandarin, the official language of the country and the language everyone had to learn at school, and thought of their own dialect as the 'purest' form of the Chinese language and, of course, the only one worth speaking.

At least they were suitably impressed by the Buddha though, and Mrs. Lu had rushed to photograph it from different angles.

The Great Buddha was a massive bronze statue some thirteen meters in height and weighed in at over a hundred tons, but Penelope's favorite story about it was how it had actually been moved several meters by a giant tsunami wave many centuries before, which when you looked at it seemed an almost impossible feat. Japan was occasionally hit by these massive waves, like in the great disaster in 2011, which had hit the Tohoku region and resulted in a major nuclear incident which they were still dealing with, but when you looked around today, something like that happening just seemed surreal.

The truth was that it was far closer to reality than most people cared to think about.

Although Kamakura or the coast near Tokyo had not been hit by anything like this wave for centuries, the Buddha served as a reminder to everyone in Kamakura that if you lived on the east coast of Japan you were never out of danger, and the next disaster could literally be just around the corner.

The women circled the Buddha and looked into the temple's souvenir shops and other attractions. The Great Buddha itself was hollow, and it was possible to walk inside it, so the three younger women had a moment's respite from their elderly relatives, who insisted on getting their money's worth by exploring inside the statue and taking another endless series of photographs.

Without them, Penny and Fei could talk in English with Ling, who like her mother didn't speak Japanese.

"How long have you been in Japan, Penelope?" asked Ling.

"Almost as long as that statue," joked Fei.

"That's not far from the truth," said Penelope. "A long time, anyway. Is this your first trip here?"

"No. I have been here a few times before. Mainly work stuff, however. Fei and I got together the last time for dinner. She took me to have *yakitori* somewhere," she smiled.

"Of course. I would have been surprised if she had taken you anywhere else."

Once again, the weather was hot and humid, and it was nice to get into the shade to escape it. While they had a moment, the women discussed Ling's busy life at the hospital in Shanghai, and it was while they were having this conversation that Penelope caught a glimpse of a familiar face just entering the temple grounds and called out to her.

"Eriko!"

The girl stopped and smiled when she saw Penelope walking towards her.

"Hello, Penny-*sensei*! What are you doing here?" said Eriko.

She looked completely different today without her maid's uniform and was wearing a pair of fashionably ripped blue jeans and a t-shirt.

"Oh, I'm a tour guide for the day," said Penelope, gesturing behind her to Fei and Ling, who were sitting in the shade of a large camphor tree.

"You're not working today?"

Penelope wondered if the Takahashi's, who only employed one maid, ever gave her any time off at all.

Eriko shook her head. "Actually, I got fired a few days ago," she said in a matter-of-fact way.

Penelope was shocked.

"Fired? They fired you?" she exclaimed. "Why on earth would they do that."

Eriko shrugged. "To tell you the truth, if they hadn't fired me, I would have left anyway. I've never liked working there, especially not with the old *iemoto*. He was, well… I shouldn't speak ill of the dead… but you know…" she smiled.

Penelope got the feeling that Eriko was actually quite pleased at this sudden turn of events. She couldn't imagine working for the old man either.

"Still, that's very weird. But I would have thought things might have been easier for you, especially after he er… well. Passed away…" said Penelope.

Eriko made a gesture of helplessness.

"Yeah, I thought so too. But it got worse. There's been a lot of screaming up there lately. I just got fed up with it. You were always walking on eggshells with all of them. And you never knew when someone was going to blow up again. Let's just say it wasn't a nice place to work."

"Hmmm… I understand… So did Issei fire you?"

Eriko shook her head.

"Issei? No. He's been OK with me. Issei is weird in other ways… You know he has a mental problem, don't you?"

Penelope shook her head, surprised.

"No, I did not. What's the matter with him?"

"He has a kinda, I dunno, neatness compulsion. His room, for example. All the clothes are arranged according to color. All the books are in alphabetical order. When he eats, he likes everything in separate dishes, always on the same dishes. And so on and so on. If anything gets put away out of order, he goes off his head. But he's been OK with me. I just try not to go into his room or anything," she said.

"Anyway, Haruko has been pretty upset though with them. They are always arguing about money and stuff. And it was Momoko san who fired me. It was bizarre…."

"Momoko? What on earth did you do?"

Eriko shrugged.

"To tell the truth, I have no idea. I was in the library dusting and I was putting away some books that she had left out. Anyway, she just came up behind me, snatched the book I was dusting out of my hand, and told me I was fired. No reason. Just get out of the house, they would send me my wages. That was that."

"Momoko said that?" said Penelope, stunned.

"Yep. She has quite a temper sometimes."

Penelope shook her head. "I had no idea. I'm sorry that happened to you, Eriko."

Eriko smiled. "Yeah, please don't be. It's fine, really. They are all nuts up there, so it's for the best, I think. I can always work at my mother's dress shop anyway. It's a lot less stress than working for the Takahashi's…."

"I guess so. So what brings you here?" asked Penelope.

"I'm meeting my boyfriend here for lunch. His family has a sake shop down the street. I just thought I would kill some time here," she said.

Something suddenly occurred to Penelope, and she decided to seize the chance while she had it.

"You know, Eriko san, there was something I wanted to ask you if you don't mind."

Eriko smiled. "Sure. What is it?"

Penelope took her by the arm, and they sought the shade of one of the little souvenir shops.

"Do you remember the night the old *iemoto* died? You said that Momoko and Issei were in the library?"

Eriko thought for a moment.

"Yes, that's right. They were watching TV or something."

Penelope gave her a long look. "Did you actually see them?"

"See them?" Eriko stood and thought for a long moment again.

"Um… See them… Maybe not. I heard them talking in there, though."

"Ah, OK. That's fine, then. You didn't happen to overhear what they were talking about, did you?"

113

Eriko blushed a little and fidgeted.

"Well, I shouldn't. But… yeah, I did hear a little."

Penelope gestured for her to go on.

"It was something about a pregnancy," said Eriko looking at the ground.

"A pregnancy? Who? Momoko?"

Eriko shook her head.

"No, I don't think so. I think it may be one of Issei's girlfriends. Something about her being hysterical and being pregnant. I think that's what Issei was saying."

"Wow. OK. And did you hear anything else?"

"Not really. It was a long conversation, though, they were talking in there for about an hour, and then the TV came on too. I think they were watching a movie or something. I didn't hear much else other than that. I think I went to my room. They never asked for anything, and they don't usually call me after dinner anyway, and I think Momoko told me they didn't need me for anything else that night. At least, I think it was then. But if they want something, they can always ring for me up there too, there is an intercom set up in my room and in the kitchen. Another thing I didn't like much…" she sighed.

Penelope smiled.

"I can imagine. Anyway, thanks for that. Say hi to your mother from me, OK?"

"Sure, I will."

At that moment, Fei came over and greeted Eriko and informed them that they had to be moving on to the next item on the agenda, which was lunch.

As they walked back to the station, Penelope's mind was racing over what she had just heard. Was this yet another scandal of Issei's? Did he really have a pregnant girlfriend? If he did, that would really set the cat among the pigeons after the gambling debacle. And why would Momoko suddenly fire a sweet girl like Eriko just for dusting a few of her books? In truth, she had no idea Momoko had it in her to fire anyone, and it seemed extremely out of character for her to do such a thing. And what was she fighting about with Haruko and Issei? Was their financial plight as dire as it was rumored to be?

All these things churned in her head as they walked back towards the station and the restaurant, where Auntie Chen had already ordered an entire course of staggering size which would have been enough to satisfy a dozen people for a week.

Chapter 11

Sweet Death

The second day of the Grand Tour, as Fei somewhat sarcastically called it, found Penelope too exhausted to get up and do her usual writing and almost too tired to even water the garden before she left.

The weather during the days for the last week had been especially hot for late September, and even at night it had not been much cooler. When Fei stumbled into her house, she too was complaining that it was too hot to be taking tourists around all these places, and even Auntie Chen had given in and been persuaded not to implement the full rigours of the planned schedule the previous day, which had proven all but impossible to carry out in the time that she had allowed.

Ling and her mother had stayed the night at a nearby hotel, and they had arranged to meet again back at the station at the same time as on the previous day for another round of temples and shrines and Chinese restaurants for lunch.

At 10 am, they met up with Ling and her mother again, who did not seem to be showing any ill effects from the previous day. Fei and Penelope wondered how they were coping with the heat.

"Actually," said Ling, "summer is worse in Shanghai. A lot worse. And Beijing can be like an oven. This is not so bad, and it's near the sea. I think most Chinese would find this pretty pleasant really."

"Well, at least we are going to Hase today. It should have a nice breeze if nothing else.

For today's trip out to Hase temple, they had been joined by Fujimoto-san and Momoko, who had invited them to come to the Takahashi estate later in the afternoon to experience the tea ceremony, which Ling had expressed an interest in. Her mother, Mrs. Lu, had decided that she and Auntie Chen would visit Engakujii instead, where Chief Inspector Yamada's brother had apparently been dragooned into showing them around.

"I don't know where they get the energy from, do you?" Fei remarked as they watched her aunt and Mrs. Lu striding ahead of them up the road from the station toward Hase temple. The two older women had iron constitutions and a relentless energy that put their younger relatives to shame.

"Maybe there is something to Chinese food after all," said Penelope. "They certainly are healthy. Better than me, anyway."

"I always thought my mother existed on a diet of gossip, not food," said Ling. "That's what she and her friends spend all day doing at my house, it seems. Drinking tea, eating sweets and talking, talking, talking…. It's the same every day."

As they approached the well-marked sign that led to the turnoff to Hase, Penelope spied Momoko and Fujimoto-san standing on the corner waiting for them, dressed in bright cotton *yukata*, which were much lighter and more pleasant to wear than the heavier *kimono* in hot weather. Momoko looked especially pretty in her light blue *yukata* with a butterfly design, which she had paired with a bright yellow sash. Both women also carried traditional umbrellas made of *washi* paper to fend off the sun, which was already beating down on the group.

After a round of introductions, they headed off up the little street, with their elderly relatives in the lead as usual. Just before the temple entrance, they found several small souvenir shops and disappeared from view into them. It did not seem to matter that these shops all seemed to sell the same things, as for Auntie Chen and her cousin they seemed to have some kind of a magnetic attraction, and they were unable to pass one without going in and buying something.

"I really don't know why they bother dragging us to all these temples," said Fei. "My aunt has absolutely no interest in Buddhism or history, all she wants to do is have a quick look around and then either eat something or buy more souvenirs."

"Yes, my mother is the same," said Ling. "Our house is practically heaving with all the bits of rubbish she has picked up on her travels. It's the same everywhere she goes."

After Momoko had insisted on buying them all the entry tickets, they entered the grounds. Once again, Auntie Chen proudly pushed Penelope, the Famous Professor of History, to explain what they were all about to see.

Fei and the others applauded, and Penelope gave them a brief potted history of the temple that she had Googled this morning and then led them up the path to the main Buddha

Hall and to the viewing point next to it, which had a magnificent view of the sea and the surrounding coastline.

At the top of the path, she took them in to look at the famous statue of the Eleven-Headed Kanon, resplendent in its gold leaf and already surrounded by several worshippers who were praying and offering incense.

The statue had an interesting past, and Penelope, who loved a mystery, was happy to tell the story, which even Fei was unaware of.

"The legend goes," said Penelope, as they stood in front of the giant golden Buddha, "Is that this statue is one of a pair. Two priests from Hase in Nara, on the other side of the country, came upon a great tree in the forest and carved two identical statues. The first they installed in the temple in Nara, and the other one, this one, they threw into the sea. The statue washed up in various places, and every time it was found, the people that touched it died. So they threw it back into the sea."

"Until the day it washed up here, which was obviously where it wanted to be. It became a harmless statue again and was installed here, where it looks out over the city, almost like it was caring for it," she said.

While telling the story, she looked at Momoko, who seemed to be a little withdrawn and distracted today, even though she had been talking amiably with Ling and telling her how happy she was that Ling could come to her home later.

As they walked down the hill to head to their lunch destination, Penelope fell into step beside Fujimoto-san. It took no more than a simple raised eyebrow from Penelope, and Fujimoto-san took her arm and whispered,

"I can't talk about it here. But it's not good news," the older woman said in a low voice.

Penelope nodded, and they decided to save the story for a later moment when they could be alone.

In the meantime, Momoko was busy pointing out the sights to Ling and doing her best to be a good tour guide.

"Auntie should have asked her to be the leader of this expedition. After all, she was born here, and didn't she study history too?" said Fei as they led the way to the *Red Duck*, a well-known Chinese restaurant back in the city center.

When they arrived. Penelope watched Momoko as she lifted back the *noren* curtain covering the restaurant's front door so everyone could go inside.

"Yes, she did. She loves history. Maybe auntie will give me a reprieve and pick on her from now on..." said Penelope.

As the *Red Duck* was owned by distant relatives of both Auntie Chen and her cousin, the owners seemed to have pulled out all the stops for this lunch, and for the next two hours, course after course rolled out of the kitchen and onto the huge red table they were all seated around. Penelope thought she had never seen so much food, even at Auntie Chen's.

The owners, who were a pleasant middle-aged couple, were very happy to see their long-lost relative from Shanghai and insisted on taking a stream of photographs of the happy occasion. The wife was apparently a distant cousin, and they had been regular hosts to Auntie Chen and Fei in the past. All around the table now was a constant hum of loud Shanghainese, which Ling and Fei did their best to translate for Penny and the Japanese, who didn't understand a single word of what was being said.

Towards the end of the meal, if there was an end, Penelope saw the familiar face of Chief Inspector Yamashita appear at the restaurant door, who smiled and greeted them all. The inspector had been the one to suggest to Fei that his brother give the ladies a tour of his temple, Engakuji, being one of the most famous temples in the city, and as he lived so close himself, he had volunteered to escort the older ladies to the temple where he could introduce them to his sibling.

The inspector was a welcome sight for Fei and Penelope, particularly as he was able to suggest that they should finish their lunch and move on now, rather than endure another round of tea and sweets, which the owners were now suggesting they do.

Fei jumped to her feet and proclaimed,

"Yes auntie, you really need to make a move now. Don't keep Yamashita-san waiting…" which seemed to do the trick and a few minutes later they were all saying their goodbye's outside the restaurant.

After seeing the two older women off in a taxi for their short trip to Enkakuji, where they were supposed to be taken on a tour and have tea with the abbot, the other women hailed their own taxi for the drive to the Takahashi estate where they were going to have a short demonstration of the tea ceremony. This was mainly for the benefit of Ling, although Fei also had expressed an interest, having not seen a tea ceremony since she was in junior high school.

When the taxi drew up to the main gates of the Takahashi estate, Ling was amazed.

"Wow, you live here?" she exclaimed to Momoko, looking up at the gracious old Meiji Period mansion surrounded by its extensive gardens. "It looks huge!"

"Yes," said Momoko modestly. "This is the family home. It's more of a business than a home, though, in many ways. The tea business, you know!" she exclaimed in a somewhat sarcastic tone. "It's getting a bit old. The roof leaks but we can't afford to get it fixed. That happens when you live in a one hundred and fifty-year-old wooden building. Believe me, it's got its issues. The builders said it would cost like millions of yen or something to fix."

Momoko led the way up the path, and they went around the side of the house into one of the smaller tea houses. Penelope's attention was drawn to the main tea room where Momoko's father had died, which was still locked up with the shutters closed.

"I guess it's going to be hard for her ever to go in there again," she said quietly to Fujimoto-san. "What an awful memory for her...."

Fujimoto-san agreed.

"It may not be a problem much longer," she whispered.

Penelope stared at her, surprised.

Momoko was already inside the tea house and was showing Fei and Ling the proper way to enter the room through the low *nijiriguchi* doorway.

"What do you mean?" said Penelope.

Fujimoto-san cast her disturbed look.

"Issei wants to sell the school. The house, the school, everything. Says they need the money," she whispered.

Penelope stood there with her mouth open, aghast.

"You're joking," she said.

"I'm not. Momoko told me yesterday. Apparently, they already have a buyer."

"A buyer?"

Fujimoto-san nodded. "Yes, the Inamoto school. In Ibaraki. They want to take it over."

Penelope was horrified. "Poor Momoko…" she said as they prepared to enter the tea room. "When was all this decided?"

"It's been going on for months. It's not just Issei's idea. It was his father's and Haruko's. But Issei is now fully on board with it, especially since he learned about the bowl and how much money was involved," Fujimoto-san whispered.

Penelope shook her head in disgust. They entered the tea house and took their seats in the little room where Momoko was cheerfully busying herself with the tea equipment and explaining the process to Ling and Fei.

Penelope could not get Fujimoto-san's news out of her mind. For a family as old and well-established as the Takahashi's, the act of selling and giving up the school was almost unthinkable. It would be considered tantamount to a betrayal of everything their ancestors had built over the centuries, not to mention the thousands of students the school catered for. Even for Penelope, a foreigner, the significance of such an act of abandonment in a Japanese family was shocking, let alone in a major traditional family such as this.

She was still reeling from the news when there was a knock on the tea house door, and Penelope received another shock.

Issei, now the *iemoto* of the Takahashi school, entered the room and sat next to Penelope at the end of the little row of guests watching Momoko making tea.

He greeted them all, especially Ling, who was surprised to see such a good-looking young man suddenly appear among them. Issei was dressed in a smart, light-grey linen suit and an open-necked shirt, which was a sensible choice given the weather. He looked more like a film star than the Grandmaster of a tea school.

"Hello, Penny-*sensei*... long time no see," he said to Penelope with a smile.

Penelope nodded her greetings, and Fujimoto-san gave him a short bow.

"I saw you coming from the house, so I thought I would drop in. I hope you don't mind," he asked, addressing himself to Ling, who smiled and nodded.

"This is a big honor for you, Ling-san," said Momoko with a smile. "My brother may be head of the school, but we don't see him in a tea room often...."

Issei laughed and smiled at them all.

"No, she's right, I'm afraid. I wasn't doing anything anyway, and it's a pleasure to meet you all. And I can watch all the mistakes my sister is making. That's half the fun," he said.

"Shush," said Momoko, with a pretty smile. "Or I won't give you any tea."

Issei seemed in a very good mood and chatted happily with the women, telling them a little about the school's history and the tea ceremony.

Meanwhile, Momoko handed out some moist sweets on small squares of *washi* paper with a little bamboo cutter on each and passed them down the line of guests. While they were eating, she expertly made thin tea in individual bowls and handed them out while explaining everything to Ling, who was clearly enjoying herself.

Penelope shot a glance at Issei, who had stood up.

"Please excuse me…" he said in a hoarse voice, and began to stumble to the door of the tea room.

Everybody stared at him as he swayed on his feet and then hastily slid open the little door and disappeared into the garden.

"Is he OK?" asked Fei.

"He didn't look OK. Somebody should check," said Penelope.

At that moment, they heard a horrible gargling sound coming from outside.

Ling was on her feet in an instant and rushed to the door, where she took one look outside and shouted to them.

"Get an ambulance!"

By the time the rest of them were outside, Ling and Fei, both doctors, were crouched over Issei, who was lying face up and unable to breathe.

"He's in anaphylactic shock," said Ling in the business-like voice of the Emergency room physician she was. "Does he have any epinephrine?" she shouted at Momoko.

Momoko was staring at her, stunned.

"I don't know. What's that?" she said.

"It's like a hypodermic syringe. An epi-pen. He should have one. Does he have any allergies? Like to peanuts?" said Ling.

Issei was now convulsing on the ground, his whole body spasming in agony.

Momoko suddenly seemed to snap out of her shock and turned and raced towards the house.

"I've seen this many times before. He needs that shot right now, or we could lose him," said Ling.

The next few minutes seemed to crawl by, and during this time, Issei slowly stopped convulsing and fell quiet. Fei and Ling were desperately trying to give him heart massage and clear his airways, but nothing seemed to work. Penelope and Fujimoto-san rushed to the front gates to direct the ambulance to the house and stood there nervously waiting for it to arrive.

A few minutes later, Momoko came running from the house with a small leather satchel marked with a large red cross.

Ling snatched it from her hand, ripped one of the epi-pens from the bag, and administered it in one quick, practiced movement directly into the center of Issei's chest.

Issei remained unmoving though, and the women continued to give him heart massage until they heard the sound of a siren turning into the driveway and they turned Issei over to the paramedics who had come rushing towards them.

Ling and Fei stood aside, and Fujimoto-san put her arm around Momoko, who was standing with her hands over her mouth and her breath heaving.

"I didn't know he was coming... I didn't check... the sweets... Oh my God..." she kept saying.

Momoko left in the ambulance with her brother, and the rest followed in the first available taxi to the nearest hospital.

Issei was confirmed dead an hour later.

Chapter 12

Pasta Alla Vongole

The little seaside town of Kamakura has a lot of excellent restaurants, and many specialize in Western cuisine, not just the usual Japanese dishes. Some of them are so well known that people will even make the trip from Tokyo to go there.

For Penelope, though, most of the time when she ate out, she found herself at a Japanese restaurant for some reason, maybe because the quality of the food at those was always pretty guaranteed. As any tourist will find out to their cost, just because you were in a major foodie city like Paris or Madrid, you would still probably find that at least 50% of the restaurants were actually quite bad.

This is not the case in Japan, where pretty much anywhere you walked into, at least in the larger cities, will be quite good, and the rest had standards that were through the roof. It was not for nothing that Japan has long had more Michelin-starred restaurants than France, and that fact was not wasted on a little town like Kamakura either.

However, despite having lived in Japan for more than three decades and being an overwhelmingly frequent visitor to Japanese restaurants, Penelope's culinary repertoire at home was unashamedly Western. This was the food she had grown up with, and it was hard to shake the feeling that in her family's cooking, there was the taste of home, and that gave her a sense of comfort.

She was no slouch in the kitchen herself, even if she was entirely self-taught, and had a pretty impressive collection of cookbooks and a large file of dishes she made for herself regularly, so she was more than capable of whipping up food from a number of different cultures and culinary traditions.

She had also long ago made it a point of honor as a single woman that she was not going to be one of those who 'couldn't be bothered to cook for one and thus found themselves eating either toast or some prepared food from a convenience store or supermarket every evening.

She had a large, modern oven installed in her house as one of her first acts after moving in and cooked nearly all her food from scratch, a habit which had made her many friends at the small shops around her house that she frequented to get whatever she needed, and had also enabled her to make full use of her garden for a lot of her food, especially during the summer months where she often had so much produce she was happy to be able to share it with Fei and her other neighbors.

A few days after Issei's death she had offered to cook dinner for Fei and Chief Inspector Yamashita for their regular *shogi* night, as it appeared that even the indomitable Auntie Chen was exhausted after taking her guests around for the last few days. She was also secretly glad as she could find out the latest as to what had been transpiring in this case and especially if any action was being considered with regard to Momoko or Haruko, who had now been closely linked to two unnatural deaths in the last month alone.

She got her answer within ten minutes of the Inspector arriving at her house and before the poor man had barely had a chance to have his first glass of beer.

Due to the nature of Issei's death, an autopsy had been ordered immediately to establish whether the poor man had been the victim of any unnatural causes. This had been performed by a colleague of Fei's who had been on duty that night, and Fei had only been able to see the report courtesy of the inspector that afternoon.

"It was as everyone expected," he said as Penelope poured him some more beer. "He had a severe allergic reaction to the sesame used in the sweets and died of asphyxia. He had a lifetime and clearly very severe allergy that was extremely well documented when we checked out his medical history with his doctor, who had been treating him since he was a child. The family was very careful with him at all times as there had been some close calls when he was young, so he always kept his medicine close to him, and if he went out, it was usually in his bag, and he also even had some in the glove compartment of his car just in case."

Penelope looked at her, confused.

"So why did they buy sweets with sesame in them in the first place? Why have something like that in the house?"

The chief inspector finished his beer.

"That was my first question too. I interviewed both Haruko-san and Momoko-san yesterday. The thing was that neither of them was allergic to it, nor was anyone they knew apart from Issei. From what I can gather, that type of sweet is pretty common in the tea ceremony, right Penny-*sensei*?"

he said as he finished his beer and held out his glass to Fei, who was in charge of the bottle.

"Yes, they are, that's true. I've had them a thousand times," said Penelope. "But if I had someone in the house who was allergic to them like that I would make a point of *not* buying something like that. Just in case. There are a million other *wagashi* that don't use sesame. You can even ask the vendor not to use it if you know them. And here is another point, by the way. Don't Haruko's parents own one of the most well-known *wagashi* shops in Kyoto? I'm betting that's where the Takahashi school gets all its sweets."

"That's true. I had forgotten about Haruko's family business," said the inspector.

He cleared his throat and continued.

"Anyway, here's the point, however. According to them, Issei never touched *wagashi*, Japanese sweets. A bit strange for a tea master, but he didn't really like them. He also didn't have much of a sweet tooth anyway, and when he did eat sweets, they were usually the Western type, like cake and so forth."

"He didn't like *wagashi*? That's weird in itself," said Penelope. For half of the women she knew who practiced the tea ceremony, the sweets were the reason they came in the first place.

"And also no one expected him to drop in unannounced at the tea ceremony in the first place. He hardly ever did that, and so Momoko didn't even give the sweets a second thought, which is understandable. She handed the sweets out to you first, so she had not even tasted them herself as she was the one making the tea. Maybe she would have twigged something was wrong if she had. Anyway, it's a moot point now."

"Didn't she arrange the sweets herself?" asked Penelope, "After all, it was her party."

The inspector shook his head.

"Apparently not. According to her, it was Haruko who bought all the sweets that were used at the school. Coming from a family like hers, obviously, she knows the most about it. They had a pile of different sweets in the cupboard and in the refrigerator in the kitchen, which is where they are kept. Momoko asked her to leave some out for her that morning before she left, and Haruko left them in the tea house for her. They were all bought the month before with a bunch of others from their usual vendor," he said.

"So Haruko bought sweets with sesame in them? Why would she do that?"

"Anyway," said Fei, "Bottom line, it was an accident. Issei should have known better in the first place. He assumed the sweets were safe, or he didn't think about it, and neither did Momoko, especially as he was the last person she was expecting to turn up. Momoko also claims she had no idea there was sesame in them, she just used what Haruko had left out for her."

"That sounds a bit fishy to me. Most tea masters know exactly what is in a sweet they serve. They need to know because it is part of the ceremony for the guests to ask questions," said Penelope as she served the pasta alla vongole she had been cooking.

"Yes, that's true, I guess," said the inspector. "But according to Momoko, the vendor also makes different versions of the same sweet, which all look the same. Some have sesame, others have bean paste, and there are two or three more as well. We checked with them, and she was telling the truth. The fact is, she just assumed they were the usual harmless ones they normally order. And don't forget, neither Haruko nor her had any idea Issei would turn up and eat one."

The inspector took a mouthful of pasta. "This is very good, Penny-*sensei*. We should have *shogi* here more often," he smiled.

Penelope poured them all a glass of chianti. After the first course, she gave them tiramisu, one of her mother's signature dishes, back in England when she was a girl.

"So, are you still suspicious?" said Fei in her usual teasing tone.

"Hmmm…" said Penelope. "How do we know she didn't invite him to join them? Or that Haruko didn't insist he go and see them? All the while knowing that he was going to eat something poisonous!"

The inspector and Fei gave each other an amused smile.

"Conjecture, your honor," said the inspector, in his best imitation of a trial lawyer. "Move to strike the previous question."

"Why is it just conjecture? Occam's razor, you know. Wouldn't it be simpler to assume that a man who hardly ever showed his face in a tea room would suddenly turn up uninvited? Wouldn't it be more logical that someone *had* invited him to join them?" said Penelope, who loved playing devil's advocate almost as much as Fei.

The chief inspector smiled.

"You would have made a good prosecution attorney Penny-*sensei*. But let me just put it this way, since you bring

132

up poor Occam. If you wanted to feed the poor man something that would kill him, why not just feed it to him privately? Why would you do it in front of several other people, two of whom are doctors and one an emergency ward physician who correctly diagnosed the problem in three seconds flat? He might not have even died at all," he concluded. "Then where would you be?"

Penelope had the feeling he spoke this way to his junior officers, polite but terrifyingly logical. Such a man, they all knew, was rare in the Japanese police, an original thinker who could see things in different ways.

"Maybe the person that did this wanted it done in front of witnesses. Maybe it's just less suspicious that way. And she had no idea Ling was a doctor, I think. I didn't know that myself until the morning I met her," Penelope argued.

"Well, Momoko knew she was a doctor, and she knows I am a doctor too. Don't forget we were all talking about Ling's job at lunch. So she knew about it before the tea ceremony," said Fei.

Penny finished her chianti and poured another glass for them all.

"OK. Well, why didn't he have his medicine on him? I hear people like that always carry it."

"True again," answered Fei. "But he was at home, wasn't he? Home, being the place where he had plenty of medicine…."

"So why did Momoko take so long to get it from the house then?" asked Penelope.

"And why do you have such a suspicious mind, pray? I thought you liked Momoko. Remind me not to commit a crime; you will probably be the first up volunteering to be a witness for the prosecution. A good old film that, by the way…" laughed Fei.

"That's not true. You would get away with it anyway. You can't trust the medical profession; they will always do you in during the night…" said Penelope with a smile.

The inspector coughed.

"Now ladies. Anyway, Fei, don't be so hard on her. I'm a cop, and in my profession, having a suspicious mind is a requirement for the job. I like it, actually…."

He smiled and patted Penelope's hand.

"And in answer to your question, which I also asked Momoko san, by the way," he said, frowning reprovingly at Fei. "The reason it took her so long to fetch Issei's medicine was simply that she couldn't find it. She thought it was in his bedside drawer. In fact, he kept it in a drawer in the bathroom. She couldn't find it, so she eventually remembered they had a second supply in the kitchen, so she got it from there."

"That's convenient," said Penelope archly.

The inspector ignored her and went on.

"The fact is that Issei hadn't had an attack in years, not since he was a teenager. So, he hadn't told anybody where he kept his medicine in recent times. Momoko didn't even know about the supply he had in his car, as she had never been near the vehicle since he bought it…. Oh, and one more thing, since we are on police business it seems here tonight… what's the motive for killing Issei? Why would anyone want him dead in the first place?"

They were all silent at this observation, which was perfectly valid. If the school were to continue, it would obviously be to everyone's advantage if Issei took it over, which was precisely what he had announced he intended to do. Momoko had, by all accounts, been close to her brother, and neither of them seemed to bear their stepmother any particular ill will either. When you looked at the situation as a whole, things may have run a lot more smoothly with Issei as the new *iemoto* than they had with their father, who had a well-known reputation for being bad-tempered and generally difficult to be around.

Penelope shrugged.

"I suppose so. It looks like there is an answer for everything... Maybe that's what I don't like about all this, it's so...neat. No loose ends anywhere. Or maybe we just haven't seen them yet. It's just all these little things that bother me. If her father and brother's death were murders, someone has done an excellent job of making them look natural, or at least as if no one else was involved."

"That may well be true. Contrary to popular opinion, you are not the only one at this table with a suspicious mind," said the chief inspector with a gentle smile, but you could tell he meant it.

"That's good to hear. Because I still have questions," said Penelope, undeterred.

"For example: with the father's death, why was the light switched off in the tea room? Where did he get the poison? I mean, cyanide? Where did that come from? Also, why did he leave a typed and not a written suicide note? The man could barely turn on a computer. And why did that note say so little? Is that all you would have to say before you sprang off this mortal coil? And also, back to Issei for a moment, why did he suddenly come to that tea room? What's the sudden fascination with having a bowl of tea with a bunch of middle-aged women?"

Fei rolled her eyes.

"Not the light thing again. Maybe one of the staff or someone turned it off, and you didn't notice. Maybe the bulb was blown. You were not the first person in that room, you know…. And go easy on the middle-aged thing. I am still incredibly attractive, as you well know…" said Fei with a laugh.

The inspector stood and took his plate into the kitchen.

"Those are good questions, though, Fei-san," he said as he sat down again. "And believe me, I haven't finished investigating yet. Even though they do seem to have an excuse for everything…" he said. "Now… am I beating you at *shogi* or not?"

Chapter 13

The Chattering Mind

The great monastery of Engakuji, just a short walk from Kita-Kamakura station, was a very familiar place for Penelope, not just because her friend Chief Inspector Yamashita's brother was head monk there, but because it was where she had gone regularly for many years to a class in *zazen*, the style of sitting meditation practiced in the Zen school.

She had started going here when she was about forty years old and in the middle of her busy career as a Professor of Japanese Literature at Hassei University, and she had just kept going ever since. She found it gave her life a centeredness and equanimity it had not previously possessed and also made her, oddly, not only calmer but more productive than she had been before.

One of the things that had drawn her there in the first place was because it had one of those rare classes held in English. At the time her spoken Japanese had not been quite good enough to understand all the Buddhist terminology that had been used in the Japanese-only classes, so she had opted for this one. And even though she was now fluent enough to cope with the Japanese without any issues, she had stayed with this class for over twenty years now.

Because the class was in English, it was popular with the foreign community and also with tourists wanting to learn something more about Zen, and this had enabled her to meet a great many people from all over the world, many of whom appreciated being able to talk with an old Japan hand and veteran like her about living in Japan, and not just about Buddhism.

She had also become a well-known entity at the temple, known by many of the monks, including Dokan *roshi*, the inspector's brother, who was a fluent English speaker that had often led her class, which consisted of about forty minutes of meditation, a short dhamma talk and then tea afterward. She and Dokan had become friends over the years, and she had met him not only here but also at his family home with his brother and at other venues where he had been asked to speak. She had even acted as his editor on occasion as he had previously written several books and articles on Buddhism in English.

The class that met that Thursday morning usually had about twenty people, most of whom were local regulars and some tourists, who today were a young couple visiting from Amsterdam. They met in the ancient meditation hall, where they sat cross-legged on small cushions facing a wall.

A small bell rang, and the meditation session began, during which Dokan or another monk would come around and correct their sitting posture to ensure that their back was straight, often by tapping them on the shoulder in the traditional way with a short bamboo stick called 'the rod of enlightenment.' While this may have been seen as some kind of corporal punishment by many Westerners, it was nothing of the sort, and Penelope found that over time, she welcomed this method of correction and found it greatly helped her to concentrate.

This morning she definitely felt an autumn chill in the air as she went to talk with her friend after the class was over.

Dokan was a tall, spare figure with a shaved head and small gold-rimmed glasses, but he still greatly resembled his younger brother, with whom he shared many traits. Both men were particularly acute observers of others and had an ability to listen in such a way that people felt they could trust them and usually opened up to them about their lives.

The monk was one of Penelope's oldest and closest friends, someone she knew she could confide in and who gave her good advice when needed.

"So Penny-*sensei*, Eiji tells me you have been having many adventures in the tea world lately," said Dokan, as he sat down next to her on one of the meditation cushions and arranged his robes neatly underneath him. 'Eiji' was, of course, his brother the chief inspector, but Dokan almost never used people's titles, even his own as the second most senior monk apart from the Abbot, whose shoes he was tipped to fill one day.

Penelope nodded and smiled.

"Yes, I wondered if he might have mentioned that to you," she said, uncrossing her legs and stretching them out on the little matted stage.

Dokan smiled. "I never knew *ocha* could be so... violent," he said. "I was sorry to hear about this, however. The old *iemoto* occasionally performed the tea ceremony here, and I participated a couple of times. And now the son, Issei? That was a tragedy. I prayed for his soul."

Dokan looked down and gave Penelope his usual unpretentious smile.

"That's kind of you," said Penelope. "I seem to have got mixed up in the whole thing. There are many things about the deaths that confuse me."

Dokan nodded.

"Eiji told me. He thinks you have raised some good questions. I told him you always do, though…" he smiled. "Is the boy's funeral soon, I take it?"

"It's today. At the same funeral place as his father's. I even expect a lot of the same folk will be there…."

"They will be getting used to it. Like me…" he said, observing that for many Buddhist monks, funerals were often a daily affair.

"I guess so," said Penelope.

There was a short silence between them for a moment, and the monk waited as he usually did for her to speak.

"Did you hear about the bowl? The Rikyu bowl?" she asked.

Dokan nodded. The monastery had a large tea room that was often used for *ochakai* and the like. Zen monasteries like his had been the first to adopt green tea when it had made its way from China, where the monks used it as a tonic for good health and as an aide to staying awake during long meditation sessions.

Dokan nodded and smiled.

"Oh yes, that was an amazing find. I can imagine how shocked they were to come into possession of that," he said. "I hear some builders dug it up accidentally?"

"Yes, they found it hidden in the wall of an old tea house they were pulling down."

"That must have been some moment. Have you seen it?" he asked.

Penelope shook her head. "Only photographs. The family keeps it in the bank," she said.

"I see… I always wonder why people do things like that. Rikyu would have wanted people to use it. But then again, he was a Zen priest too…" he smiled his gentle smile, and Penelope laughed.

"Not many people realize he was one of your lot," she said.

"Ah, yes. He was indeed. Without Zen, his tea ceremony makes no sense at all."

"That's true. And other people say it makes no sense with it either," she quipped.

Dokan nodded. "Well, perhaps neither have a point. That's also the Zen way…" he said. "How are the sister and the wife coping with so many deaths?"

"They seem to be all right," she said.

Dokan looked at her enquiringly. "And how about you, Penny-*sensei*? How are you coping?"

Penelope always had the feeling the monk was looking straight through her.

She sighed and turned up the palms of her hands.

"I'm probably just being stupid," she said quietly. "I should just go to the funeral and get on with things."

Dokan nodded. "I can tell you that I think that would be a good idea," he said calmly. "Things will make themselves clear in time. They always do…."

Penny looked at him. "If I could only know for sure that was true, I would die happy," she smiled.

The monk laughed too.

"This is what we call mind-chatter Penny-*sensei*. This is why we do *zazen*, to stop the mind from always talking to us. It never does any good to listen to it, and if you don't...eventually, it will stop talking, and everything will become clear. Silence is the answer. In all things," he said.

"This sounds like one of your dhamma talks," she smiled.

Dokan spread his arms wide. "Of course, it's my job, you know... everything will be what it will be. Your job is to accept that. Not try to change it. Just to let it be."

She nodded. "What about justice, though? Shouldn't we try to get that?" she asked.

"Justice is a delusion. But don't worry, my brother doesn't get that either," he smiled. "We all come to understanding in our own way and in our own time. Let's leave it at that. In the meantime, indulging in worry or an endless dialogue about it is nothing to be gained. If you leave it alone, it will become clear, like water. The more you stir it with a stick, the muddier it gets."

Penelope nodded. The monk invited her in for tea, but she told him that she had to go to the funeral and that she didn't have time today. She would take him up on it next time, she promised.

Dokan walked her down to the main gate of the temple just near the road, and they bowed to each other. He watched her walk up the road to the little station which would take her back into the city.

She thought about chatter.

She kept seeing the same scene playing itself out, over and over.

There were two people, talking in a library. Momoko and Issei, with the curious maid Eriko, passing by the door. They had told her she was not needed further that night. Who had told her that? Momoko probably. Still, she had hung around and heard them speaking after dinner. Probably she had been clearing up the dinner things, and you had to walk past the library door to go to the kitchen. Yes, that was how she had heard things.

They had all had dinner together that night. And then Papa had left. Where was he? Had he gone to his study? Maybe. Maybe that was when he had typed out his suicide note. But he had been in a very good mood at dinner?

She shook her head. It didn't make sense. Still the chatter filled her mind.

People in the library, talking, talking. Momoko and Issei. What were they talking about? Issei's girlfriend, that was what. Issei had got a girl pregnant. She was hysterical. Was she going to make a scene? Was she going to go to the newspapers? The gutter press, the weekly magazines?

Issei seemed to attract scandal like a barbeque attracted flies. First, he had been in debt to gangsters, and his father had paid them off. Now this poor girl. Did she want money too? Probably. And would their father pay to hush it up?

She nodded to herself.

Of course, he would. But maybe it had been the last straw for him. Perhaps he could not live to see his life, his ancestor's memory tarnished in this way and even destroyed.

Was that why he had done it?

Then why had he been in such a good mood at dinner?

Who had told her that? Eriko had. Momoko had.

Chatter, chatter, chatter.

She looked down the road at the ancient steps that led up to Engakuji. The name meant 'Perfect Enlightenment". Thinking about things now, that was the last thing she felt.

And yet.

Somewhere, maybe as the monk had been speaking to her, she felt a little ray of light dawn in the back of her mind, and she knew at last she was on to something.

If only she could see what it was.

It was strange, she often thought, that whenever she left this place, she knew she would come back, that it was like a kind of second home to her. She wondered if, in some past life, it had been.

====================

She realized how little she had spoken to Haruko that day as the funeral drew to a close.

She had known her for over fifteen years, ever since she had come to Kamakura to marry her much older husband, but she could recall only a very few conversations, and all of them had been short and fairly meaningless. Penelope wondered if this was the moment to change that.

Haruko was a strong, intelligent, and good-looking woman now in her late forties. She had been engaged to someone else once before, but it had not worked out, and her family was overjoyed when the chance came for her and them to make a match with someone of the *iemoto's* stature in the tea world, which, as a major *wagashi* vendor, was also their world.

Haruko was no foolish girl, however. She had gone to Kyoto University, the nation's second most prestigious school, studied pharmacy and chemistry and had a master's degree. After graduation, she had gone on to work for a big Japanese pharmaceutical company as a researcher and had been forging a career there apparently when marriage in the form of the *iemoto* of the Takahashi School and huge pressure from her family had put an end to all that and turned her basically into what was called an *okami-san*, the wife of someone who looked after an inn or a sumo-stable. Her job now was to look after the interests of the Takahashi School and its hundreds of students, and to ease her husband's role as he led the school forward.

As such, she was nothing more than a glorified housewife, and she didn't even have children to add a distraction. Just two step-children, neither of whom she seemed particularly close to.

Penelope wondered how she really felt about that.

After the funeral, she stood next to Haruko and Momoko as they farewelled the guests. Momoko, stately and refined in a black dress and pearls, was holding her brother's ashes, which were in a small urn wrapped in a white cloth, while Haruko was bowing and giving her thanks to those who had attended.

When the last guest had left, she and Haruko had shared a taxi together, and Haruko had unexpectedly asked her to come in for a drink when they had arrived at the estate on the way to her home.

Perhaps she just wants someone to talk to, she thought.

Haruko led the way into the library and threw her veil and hat onto the sofa.

"Whisky?" she said, "I'm having one. I think I deserve one after today."

Penelope was surprised. She didn't even know Haruko drank. In any case, she was also in the mood for something stronger than tea herself, and so she happily agreed.

"I'm not surprised. Yes, I'll have one with you, thanks," she said.

Haruko poured some Scottish malt into two very expensive-looking heavy crystal glasses and then threw herself down on the sofa.

"Well, cheers," she said, raising her glass. "Here's to Issei."

"To Issei," Penelope raised her glass, and they both drank.

"I wanted to thank you…." Haruko said, leaning forward and clasping her glass in both hands. Penelope noticed her hair, which she wore in a short bob, was a lustrous black and her skin was like a woman twenty years her junior, white and unblemished by any wrinkle. She seemed hardly to have aged a day from the pretty young bride she had been all those years before.

"I know you were there with Issei at the end. And you were also one of the first to see my husband," she sighed.

"We seem to be keeping you busy with funerals lately…" she said with a wry smile.

Penelope nodded. "If there is anything I can do… you know. If you need someone to talk to…."

Haruko waved her offer away politely. "I'm OK. But thank you. You and Fujimoto-san have been good friends and supporters for many years. I know that. Particularly for Momoko. It was very hard for her to lose her mother so young. And now all this as well… It just never seems to end, does it?"

"I'm sorry for her too. Losing her brother so soon after losing her father… it's just not fair. She must blame herself too, I think…."

Haruko finished her drink. "Issei… I don't know what he was thinking. He knew full well that tea sweets were dangerous, he almost died as a boy eating them. I know… I was there. We would have lost him a long time ago if I hadn't injected him that time. Maybe that's why he never touched them, except if he went to a tea ceremony, and even then, he always checked first. I can't believe he just went and did that. So reckless…" she said, and put her head in his hands.

"He certainly had his problems, poor boy. Momoko told me about the gambling."

Haruko nodded miserably.

"It's true. That almost killed his father. Maybe it did in the end… I don't know…."

She sighed again.

"Sometimes, I think this family is cursed. I'm not the only one who has this opinion, you know. My husband said it often enough too… Issei was a time bomb, he often said. Maybe he was right."

There was silence between them for a while.

"Did he know about the girl? There was a rumor…."

Penelope was pr*obi*ng, she knew, and she felt bad even mentioning it.

Haruko looked up, startled.

"What girl?"

Penelope looked down.

"I'm sorry. I shouldn't have said that. It was just a rumor, probably completely untrue. I'm sorry," she said, feeling deeply ashamed of herself.

Haruko got up and offered her another drink, which she refused.

"Issei and a girl?" she smiled slightly. "That would have been good news, I think. That was the other issue his father wanted hushed up… This family…. God…."

"What issue was that?"

Haruko smiled and swirled the golden liquid in her glass. "Issei… was gay. He wasn't going to hostess clubs, you know. He was going to gay clubs in Shinjuku. Had been even when he was in high school. Everyone knew it, too… that was the real scandal as far as his father was concerned. If there *had* been a girl in the picture, I think he would have been delighted!"

Chapter 14

After the Funeral

At that moment, the library door opened, and Momoko entered, holding the embroidered white bag containing her brother's ashes, which she placed gently on a table.

"I think I will have a drink as well…" she said.

Haruko got up at once and poured her a glass of whisky.

"Are you all right?" asked Penelope.

"Sure," Momoko nodded calmly. "I'll be fine."

She was still dressed in her black dress and pearls, as they all were that evening, and although she looked somewhat pale and strained, her voice and carriage showed an inner serenity and strength.

She took off her hat and veil, threw them on the table, and, unpinning her hair, shook it loose, causing it to ripple like a long dark waterfall to her waist. In so doing, she became not the mourning and serious woman she had looked when she entered but the young, more cheerful girl they knew.

"Why do funerals have to be so formal and ghastly?" she said as she took a small sip of her whisky and stared into the glass. "I'm sure I don't want one when I die. Please feel free *not* to do that for me. It just makes the whole thing worse rather than better. It's bad enough having to lose someone, then you have to go through all this tedious formality that almost seems calculated to make everyone feel worse. Better to just be done with it…."

Penelope looked down.

"I know. It's very trying… I guess it's more for other people than for those you have lost…" she said.

Haruko said nothing and just stared ahead into space. It was hard to know what she was thinking or feeling or if she was just numb to the whole thing by now.

Momoko nodded and reached out and held Penelope's hand.

"It was good of you to come. You are always there for me," she said.

Penelope gave her hand a slight squeeze.

"Of course. Fujimoto-san has been very worried too."

Momoko gave a small smile and looked around her like the room had changed somehow, and she could not understand why.

"First mother, then Papa, now Issei…." she said quietly.

Haruko nodded. "It does feel like that, doesn't it…"

There was silence for a while.

"Have you given any thought to the school?" Penelope said, trying to change the subject.

Momoko sighed and nodded. After her brother's death she had inherited his share of the estate and would now have to be the decision maker in the school's future.

"It will have to be sold as planned," said Haruko sadly. "We cannot possibly keep it going by ourselves."

Penelope looked at her and put her glass down on the table.

"It's such a shame. After so long too… but maybe it is for the best," she said.

Momoko coughed, and they both looked at her.

"Actually, it will not be sold. I am going to run it myself," she said.

Her voice was clear and business-like, and in her eyes you could see she was adamant.

Haruko sighed. "Momoko… you can't. We can't…" she said in a pleading voice.

Momoko took a swig of whisky and put her empty glass on the table with a bang.

"I will not lose the school, not after nearly three hundred years. We will keep it, and we will make it work," she said forcefully.

"And who will be *iemoto*?" asked Haruko incredulously.

Momoko stared at her, her eyes hard and unflinching.

"I will, of course. There is precedent in our history to have a woman as an *iemoto*. It is mine by right."

Haruko stared at her, unbelieving. "Momoko… you don't know what you are saying. Your father made the decision to sell, and your brother agreed with it. The Inamoto family has agreed to it. What do you think I have been doing all these months meeting with them? You cannot just change your mind like this!" she said loudly.

Momoko was silent for a moment, and then she seemed to gather herself and cleared her throat.

"I *never* agreed to it. I told you all that I did not agree, and was ignored. But… I will not be ignored now. The school belongs to me, not you, and certainly not to the Inamoto family. It will stay as it is. And *that* is my final word on the matter," she said adamantly and glared at Haruko with a ferocity that Penelope had never seen before.

"I should leave…" said Penelope. She tried to stand, but Momoko put her hand on her arm to stop her, and she fell back into her seat.

"No, you should stay and hear this. I want you to stay…" she said in a more gentle tone.

"Momoko… this is your family business. You should discuss it privately," Penelope said, but Momoko continued to hold onto her arm.

Haruko looked at Momoko and then at the floor like she had been slapped.

"Momoko, we are in debt," she said without looking up. "We are losing money daily, and it is getting worse. You know this. What else can we do? Even if you sold the bowl, it would not be enough…."

Momoko sat bolt upright, and Penelope felt the grip on her arm tighten.

"The bowl will *never* be sold, and neither will the school. We will just run things better. We can use the bowl to raise money as well. Anyway, I will not waste my time discussing this further with *you*… You are not a Takahashi. This is no longer your affair," she hissed at her stepmother icily.

Haruko stood up in a fury and stormed out of the room, slamming the door behind her.

Penelope stared at her.

"Momoko…," she whispered.

Momoko stood and calmly poured herself another drink.

"One for the road?" she said, offering the bottle to Penelope, who waved the offer away.

"Very well, I shall drink alone. I'm getting used to doing that, and maybe in the future there won't be any choice…" she said sadly and sat down next to Penelope again.

"I will organize an *ochakai* for next month, and I will announce to the membership that I am the new *iemoto* in the next few days. I hope I can count on your support." she looked inquiringly at Penelope, who nodded.

"Of course you do. You know that. We will all support you if this is what you want to do."

"It is," she said clearly. "I know she's right about the debt. I know she's right that we should sell. But we are not going to do that. We are going to carry on, that's what we have done for hundreds of years. It is what we are going to do now. And we can use the bowl too. I'm going to put it on exhibition and use it at *ochakai* and raise money with it. Do you know what a tea practitioner would pay to hold it in their hands for even a minute?" she said, and her eyes flashed darkly.

"I suppose that's true," Penelope admitted.

Whatever you thought about Momoko and her abilities to run the school, she had a point. The only artifact in the world made by the founder's own hands in private ownership was a huge draw in the tea world. There were many obsessed collectors and tea people who would pay absolutely any amount of money to own such a thing or just hold it for a moment. Managed properly, it could indeed save them from their financial problems.

Momoko bowed her head, and they sat there silently for a moment, and then Penelope made her excuses.

"Momoko, it's late. I think you should get some rest. Me too, for that matter."

Momoko saw her to the door, and Penelope walked down the driveway in the moonlight with the taste of fine whisky and something like revulsion in her mouth.

It had been a bad moment, and although she had been glad to be able to support Momoko, she felt sorry for Haruko and the way she had been treated. Now it had become clear that rather than having an affair, which had been presumed, Haruko had been negotiating the sale of the school to the wealthy Inamoto family on behalf of her husband. Probably he would have been loath to participate in such a negotiation given his heritage. No. He had sent Haruko off to do his dirty work to save them from ruin.

And Issei? Of course, he would not have wanted to become *iemoto,* that would have been the last thing on his mind. To get his hands on all the money after his father's death and spend it would have been a dream for him, presuming there was any left to be had once they cleared their debts.

She walked for a way down the darkened road leading back to Kamakura station, and waved down a passing taxi to take her on the short journey to her house.

"*Families,*" she thought. "*Families and their secrets.*"

She sighed quietly, and the driver looked at her in his rear-view mirror but said nothing. A woman dressed like her, obviously coming from a funeral. She must be sad, he thought.

=====================

That night she had a dream.

There was an old ghost story, one she had once translated from a group of old tales called the *ugetsu monogatari*, or the *Tales of Moonlight and Rain*. Ever since she had read the story, she had often had this dream. The story went like this:

Once upon a time, there had been a warrior who had gone away to war and had been separated for years from his wife and child. Finally, the war had ended and he had been allowed to return home, where he found his house, just as it had been, and his wife and child waiting for him. They were overjoyed to see him, and after a night of celebrating with his family, he fell into a deep sleep.

When he awoke, however, all was changed. He was lying in an overgrown ruin in the pale dawn light, and when he stood and looked about him, he found that he had been sleeping on his wife's grave.

Whenever Penelope had this dream, the characters changed. Sometimes she was the wife, and sometimes she was the husband. Occasionally Fei would feature as the wife, or one of the neighborhood mothers and their child would take the roles.

It was a tableau about loss, neglect, how things changed whether you liked it or not, and how loss was inevitable. There was also something about the story that she liked also, and that was that maybe, in some other realm, perhaps a realm of imagination or perhaps some other dimension, we could continue happily enjoying the life we had, and that it would not be taken away by the inexorable river of change and time. And that in that world, love would be able to find its way back to you, and you to it.

Tonight, Momoko had been the ghost of the warrior's wife, and Issei had been the long-absent husband. And when he awoke, Issei knew that Momoko had left him forever, just as he had left her long ago.

She slept late, and in the morning she found a note from Fei on the kitchen table saying that she had already been and watered the garden, as it was supposed to be hot again today.

She made some coffee and took it into her study, where she had been editing an article for an old colleague, which was on the Edo Period poet Rengetsu, one of the great women haiku periods of the late eighteenth century.

One of her simple yet poignant poems stared up at her that morning as she sat down to look at the document.

I await my beloved
who is not yet here.
The moon in the pines
and voice of the wind
provoke my longing.

She often wondered if she and Rengetsu had something in common. They were both writers, both single women trying to live in Japan. They both had their emotional problems and their issues to work through. She would have bet, if it had come to a crisis, that Rengetsu would have coped with things with more calmness and equanimity than she did. After all, she had seen war and plague and fire, lost everything and made pottery and poems for a living. And yet she never complained and found beauty in everything around her.

Perhaps Momoko was going to be like that too. She would go down fighting with her ship, a woman alone against the rest of the world.

She wished her luck. At least her heart was in the right place, and she was trying to defend a legacy passed down to her by generations of her tea master ancestors. There was something in that she admired.

Later that morning, she found Fei had returned and was sitting with a cup of coffee and her newspaper and blowing her usual smoke rings out over the ruin of the tomato plants that were trying to hang on to their little trellis on this late September day.

Penelope made herself some more coffee and joined her.

"How was the funeral?" said Fei, looking up from her paper.

"Sad, as you would expect. He was so young, after all. Twenty-five… I mean, what is that, twenty-five? You are just starting your life then…."

"Where were you at twenty-five?" asked Fei.

Penelope thought for a moment. "Er… still finishing my doctorate, I think. Living in a very ratty old flat in Highgate, quite close to the cemetery where they buried Karl Marx… tutoring for a living. No money…" she smiled.

Fei smiled too. "The good old days. I had just graduated and started working for the government. Also, no money…" she said. "And what about Momoko? And Haruko?"

Penelope told her the story as to what had transpired the previous evening.

Fei was aghast. "Momoko? *Iemoto*? You're kidding, right? I thought she would be in a short skirt running around Harajuku..." she said. Harajuku was a famous shopping area in Tokyo, beloved of young girls.

"Well, apparently not. She seemed pretty determined to me," said Penelope.

Fei sighed. "Well, now I've heard everything. So when is all this about to transpire?"

"Soon, I think. She plans to notify all the members, and I guess all the other supporters of the change in the next few days. Issei never got around to that, so no one was formally notified of the change that was supposed to take place after the father died. And the father never formally appointed him as his heir either," said Penelope.

Fei looked at her over the top of her paper. "Because he was gay? I wondered, actually... he was always a bit *too* good looking," she smiled.

"Yes, I know what you mean. Still, after all those stories I got told about him being a playboy, etc., I was a bit surprised. And then there was that story Eriko told me... she must have got that wrong, I guess."

"I suppose so. Still, that must have gone down like a lead brick with Papa. He was a died-in-the-wool conservative if ever you met one."

"True. Usually, someone in his position and at his age, you know, in his seventies, would have already designated an heir to take over. I guess everyone just presumed it would be Issei, though." said Penelope. "Anyway, there is nothing to say a woman cannot be an *iemoto*. It happens in other schools in other arts and things. I say good luck to her."

Fei nodded. "I see. So does this mean she is off the hook as far as you are concerned for murdering half of Kamakura?" she said with a wry smile.

Penelope was quiet for a while.

,"It does seem unlikely that she would be doing any killing. I mean, what does she have to gain? A bankrupt school that's up to its eyeballs in debt, and then having to explain to all your members that you, a woman, are going to take it over. You are going to get some blowback from a lot of the more conservative folk in the tea world for that," she said.

"I bet you would. That crowd is nothing if not catty old gossips," said Fei. "Give me *shogi* anytime…."

"Right… *shogi*…" smiled Penelope. "That would be the game where they have separate men's and women's competitions and separate men's and women's titles… and why is that again?"

"Because it's Japan. And most *shogi* players are guys who think they are invincible. That's why it's so nice to beat them. Besides, chess is the same. Men grandmasters and women grandmasters…." said Fei.

"True. I could never understand that," said Penelope.

"Neither could I. Most of those guys are not even that good…" she grinned evilly. "Anyway, I agree. Good luck to Momoko. At least she has her bowl, too… she can always flog that to some demented old tea nutter. No shortage of them running around," said Fei as she returned to her newspaper.

Penelope stared across the garden at a big blue butterfly attempting to land on the passionfruit trellis. In her dream, Momoko, the warrior's wife, had been making tea for her newly returned husband in a black tea bowl, and offering it to him to drink, her pale face wreathed in shadow and moonlight.

Chapter 15

A Visit to the Library

Penelope had always had an affinity, naturally enough, with libraries and had been a frequent visitor to the Kamakura Central Library in the Onaricho area to the west of Kamakura station for more years than she could remember. It was not that the library, which was relatively small by some standards, had any significant value as a research hub, but simply because she just liked being around the books and exploring all the different sections to see what they had. During her free days, she liked to come here and take things out and read them at the little desks if there was one free, and she often found in the books that she saw something that took her in different directions and gave her ideas for the books she was writing.

Libraries were probably the thing she missed most about living in Japan, as they had always featured large in her life in some way or other. Some of her earliest memories involved being taken to the local library not far from where she lived each week by her mother and her grandmother, who made a weekly shopping trip to Oxford, where she had grown up. She had her own library card before she had even gone to school and spent countless hours in the local library reading everything in sight. Yet, even after going on to Oxford University, she still visited the old library in her village whenever she returned for the holidays.

That had all changed when she had come to Japan, however.

It was not that Japan was short on good libraries, as the Japanese were one of the most literate, book-buying populations on the planet and every town in the country seemed to boast a local library.

It was simply that, even though she had managed to learn the written and spoken language to a fairly high level of fluency, she still only read Japanese with difficulty and with nothing like the fluency and understanding of nuance that she had in her native language. This fact just tended to make reading in Japanese a chore and not something she did much for enjoyment. That, and the almost total lack of English books in most places, made going to the library something she did now for the pleasure of the atmosphere and research rather than for the joy of finding something good to read at home.

It had been raining as she had left the house, and all four of her cats had given up on any outdoor activities that day and were sprawled in their favorite haunts. Biscuit and Coco particularly tended to favor the entranceway to her house and to curl up on top of the shoebox, and this is where she found them as she left the house that day to pursue an idea that had been brewing in her mind for a few weeks now at the library, where she was hoping to track down some more information on the history of the Takahashi School. It was a reasonable assumption that the library might hold some more information about one of the town's leading families, and she was on pretty good terms with the head librarian, Takamura-san, who was also an occasional visitor to Fujimoto-san's tea circle and whom she knew she could rely on for help in finding out more.

Today a light autumn rain fell as she walked through the little streets to her destination, which made her happy. She had always felt that walking through Kamakura in the rain was one of the great pleasures of living in the city. The old town, particularly the area near Kita-Kamakura and the great temple of Meigetsu-in was especially beautiful, and the best season to visit it was always the rainy season in June when the mists lay thick upon the hills and the petals of the famous hydrangea there shone their most beautiful colors.

Penelope liked any day she could walk around the town in the rain, and found herself at her destination a little sooner than she would have liked. Outside the library, which looked more like a block of flats than a local government building, she joined the short queue of library regulars, mainly elderly folk who waited each morning for the library to open so they could go in and claim their usual desks and then pick up where they had left off the day before as to whatever they were researching or just browsing. In the fierce days of summer particularly, a lot of older people came to spend the day in the library simply because it was air-conditioned and maybe just made a comfortable change of scene from their houses, and this was something she could quite understand. The library even boasted a room where you could eat your lunch, a place that a lot of these regulars made good use of.

The library was closed on Mondays but opened promptly at 9.30 am every other day, and the first person she had seen on entering it had been Takamura-san, who gave her a friendly wave from behind the counter, where she was being suddenly swamped by a line of elderly people and students returning their books.

Penelope waited until she was free, and then they retreated into her little office, where Takamura-san made her a cup of coffee.

The head librarian was a slender, almost bird-like woman in her late fifties who had worked in the central library for over thirty years, including before it had shifted from its old location, which had been an old Meiji Period mansion that had seen better days and had also had an extreme case of rot spread throughout its wooden structure. She still wore her hair long, and her half-glasses swung from a long gold chain around her neck which seemed to scream 'librarian' if you didn't actually know what she did for a living.

"The Takahashi School?" she said as she passed Penelope her mug of coffee. "Hmmm… I'm sure there is some information about that. Have you tried the section on the tea ceremony? Didn't I read recently that the old boy died? And the son? Was that them?"

"Yes, I'm afraid so, it was them. It's all very strange, I'm afraid. And yes, I've been to the tea ceremony section before, but there was not much there. I wondered if you might have like a history of the school though, maybe in a journal article or something in another related book?" asked Penelope.

Takamura-san put her pen behind her ear and took a sip of her coffee, which she seemed to drink non-stop throughout the day.

"We might do. It may be something on microfiche downstairs... was there anything specific you wanted to know? Are you writing a book on the tea ceremony now?" she asked with a smile. "It's about time if you are...."

Penny shook her head.

That's something I definitely want to do one day, but it's not going to be now. I have a pile of other stuff on my plate at the moment. No, what I want to know is about the past *iemoto*. Particularly I'm interested in the female *iemoto*."

Takamura-san raised her eyebrows. "Female *iemoto*? In a tea school? That'd be a first. I'd like to know about that myself..." she said.

She turned to a big computer which took up half the space on her desk.

"Let's see what we have." She spent a few minutes tapping away on her keyboard and making notes.

"Can you believe we still use these bloody dinosaurs here?" she said, gesturing to the computer. "I mean, seriously old... my phone has better software and is fifty times faster. And the record system here... well, you know...."

Penelope nodded her agreement and sighed. Everyone knew that the internet had been the death knell for libraries worldwide these days. Funding had been cut across Japan and indeed everywhere else due to the steep fall in people actually using their services, particularly young people, many of whom had never been inside a public library in their lives, even though they offered quite a range of online services, including movies and music for free. It was obviously not enough of a draw, however.

"OK. I think we have something here," she said after a while. Someone wrote an article on the school many years ago, a German researcher. It's on microfiche like I thought. You want to have a look?" said Takamura-san.

They made their way upstairs to an old row of microfiche machines, and Takamura-san found the reel they were looking for and inserted it into the machine.

"We don't have the money to digitalize all this stuff, and we probably never will. Anyway, you know what to do. If you have any trouble copying it, let me know. Sometimes this old equipment is a bit tricky. I'll leave you to it. Let me know when you finish. I will try and see if we have anything else."

As a student in the early 70s, Penelope was more than familiar with microfiche and the clumsy old machines that had been regarded as state-of-the-art back in her day and which had slowly been phased out in universities as their contents had been digitalized. You could still find them in many libraries and newspapers however, even though most undergraduates in the internet age had never heard of one, let alone seen one.

Penelope thanked her and sat down to scroll through the articles until she found the one she wanted, which was indeed by a German historian called Fredrich Neumann, and written back in the 60s for a magazine on Asian studies and looked like it might have been part of a thesis. Her German was not very good, but she could generally understand what was written in several European languages, even if her spoken German was limited to saying *beer bitte* and a few other words she had picked up during the one month she had spent years ago researching a book in Frankfurt.

Finally, towards the end of the article, she found what she had been looking for: a list of the *iemoto* of the Takahashi School, dating back to its founding in the seventeenth century.

And there it was.

Sure enough, in the mid-nineteenth century, one in the 1830' and another in the 1870s, were two female names listed as the head of the school, one Takahashi Saya, and another Takahashi Suiko. Both had been *iemoto* for about ten to twenty years, and both had passed on the title to men, presumably their sons, although adoption had been a common practice in Japan for over a thousand years, so they may not have been blood relations.

It wasn't much information, but now, armed with names and dates, she was in a much better situation to find out more, which would undoubtedly be in Japanese.

She put her money into the little slot and hit the 'Print' button, and waited until the old machine finished rumbling and shaking and finally churned out a less than clear shot of the page of the article she needed.

Back downstairs again, she showed her findings to Takamura-san.

"Well, I'll be damned. I will start believing in unicorns next. A woman in charge of a tea school all that time ago..." Takamura-san muttered as if to herself. She then passed a couple of volumes in Japanese over to Penelope.

"These may have some more information too, so have a look. They go into some local history on the Tea Ceremony in Kamakura. One was written by one of the local history buffs, who might still be hanging around somewhere...."

Penelope smiled. She knew that most of the head librarian's headaches were caused by old-age pensioners with nothing else to do, who wanted to research the most bizarre topics she had ever heard of in the vast amount of free time they now had.

"That wouldn't surprise me either," laughed Penelope. "I see them gathered here for your services every morning…."

The librarian made a face.

"I think half the time it's because they are just too tight-fisted to turn on the air-conditioning in their houses… or pay to use the internet…" she said. "Still, a customer is a customer, beggars can't be choosers…" she said with a smile.

Penelope thanked her and wandered over to one of the free desks to look at the material she had found. It was not that she distrusted what Momoko had told her, it was simply something that had been nagging at the back of her mind, something that she could not quite put her finger on.

Momoko had mentioned these two women *iemoto* on at least two occasions now, and it was clearly some kind of reference to the fact that she was just as qualified and entitled to have taken over the school as *iemoto* as her brother or anyone else had been. The question, though, was less that she had been aware of this particular fact about her family history than that she had been so emphatic about it. It was this that had bothered Penelope for some reason.

She browsed through the books that Takamura-san had provided. The first one had a short chapter on the history of the school, mainly focused on the more recent events of the twentieth century and the post-war period, and talked about the school's connection to the royal family during the early part of the century when a few of the *iemoto* had been tutors in the tea ceremony to various female members of the royal family, which was very important to them. Tea masters from the more important schools, such as the largest Urasenke School in Kyoto, had frequently married minor royalty, and even now, there was a strong connection to the imperial family, who had always patronized the tea ceremony in one way or another since its inception over six hundred years ago.

The second book, *A History of the Kamakura Tea Ceremony*, had more information on the development of the tea ceremony in the Kamakura area during the mid to late Edo Period, which was the period of the two women that Penelope was interested in.

She opened the front of the book and found it was indeed a short, self-published volume by one Shimada-san Yasuhiro, whom the book listed as being a resident of Kamakura and having been born in 1942.

Was he still alive?

Penelope looked around the library at several of the elderly men hanging around looking at the various newspapers and magazines and wondered if it might even be one of them. It was just the sort of place you might be able to find him, she thought optimistically.

She decided to continue her research at home, went to the main desk, checked out the books she had been given, and said her farewells to Takamura-san, who was engaged in stamping books at the counter again.

She put the books into her bag and was making her way to the door when something caused her to look down one of the rows of shelves she was passing.

In front of her was a little sign marked with the word:

'DRAMA'

On instinct, she stopped and made her way down the row of shelves. The books were all in Japanese, but there were many translations of foreign plays, perhaps even more than Japanese plays.

It took her a little searching, but finally she found what she was looking for. It was a slim white volume with the words:

STOPPARD, TOM.

Who's Afraid of Virginia Woolf.

She had seen this book in the Takahashi library, sitting by itself on top of the other copies of Momoko's mother's collection of plays. Had her mother been in this play? Or had she just read it at school like Penelope herself had? And was this the book in Eriko's hand when she had been so quickly and without any warning fired from her post?

She realized as she held the little volume in her hand that something had bothered her about this book since the moment she had first seen it. Perhaps it was just that she was familiar with the play, as it was a famous and frequent item on many literature curriculums at British high schools and universities. She also remembered seeing it on stage and watching the famous Richard Burton and Elizabeth Taylor adaption of it on screen, which she had found so riveting in its casual cruelty as a student. Like so many others, she had often wondered just how much of Burton and Taylor's tempestuous marriage was reflected in the piece.

But perhaps it was something else.

She returned to the counter, checked out the play, and was soon outside in the misty morning again.

The rain had stopped, and she walked back through the quiet streets towards the main train station again as a warm wind shook the last droplets from the leaves.

Chapter 16

The Ancestral Line

A few days later, they met outside a little cafe called *Mishima* they both knew, just off the main shopping street near Kamakura station.

Shimada-san Yasuhiro was a slight, immaculately dressed older gentleman with short white hair and gold framed glasses. He wore freshly pressed navy-blue slacks, a checked shirt, and a blue jacket for their meeting, and gave the impression that he was a person who valued the civilized ways.

He had been very easy for Penelope to track down, as the idea of consulting with Fujimoto-san had occurred to her, and as luck would have it he was an old friend whom she had helped in his research for his book on the Kamakura tea ceremony. And, of course, she still had his phone number.

They sat down, and Shimada-san ordered a latte and informed her he was more than happy to help her with her inquiries.

"How did you start writing about Kamakura?" Penny asked. "You seem to have produced quite a lot of work on the subject."

Penelope had checked him out a little online, and a quick search had produced more than a dozen of his short self-published books on all sorts of different topics, from works on Zen Buddhist temples, famous Kamakura writers and artists, battles that had taken place in the area, the Kamakura shogunate, Dogen Zenji who had founded Engakuji temple and several more. He had even heard Penelope's name and was quite familiar with Hassei, her old university, as he often made use of its library and was friends with a few people in the History Department.

Shimada-san waved away the compliment and briefly told her his story.

After retiring as an English teacher from a high school in Tokyo, he returned to his old family home to care for his aging mother and then embarked on a second career as a writer on local history. He was a member of the Kamakura Historical Association, but he published all his work himself, simply as a hobby and for whoever wanted to read it. If they didn't, it was no matter, he explained, he just liked writing and researching.

Penelope liked him at once. He had kind, smiling eyes, a natural curiosity about everything historical, and an extensive knowledge not only of the city but also of Japan itself.

"I always wanted to be a historian, actually. But we weren't well off, and my father insisted I go into teaching, so I just ended up teaching English for forty years! And then, you know, marriage, and two kids that are grown up now, of course. And I am so old now, I am kind of 'living history' myself…" he laughed.

He certainly didn't look his age, which was eighty, and Penelope told him so.

"When you have as many grandkids as I do, you age more quickly..." he said, smiling.

Eventually, they got to the point of their meeting.

"I was wondering what you could tell me about the Takahashi School if you knew much about that," Penelope asked.

Shimada-san san put down his coffee cup and cleaned his glasses with a spotless white handkerchief.

"Ah yes... that's been in the news lately, hasn't it? Unfortunate business. I met the old *iemoto* once, you know. My late wife was a school member, and so was my mother. They were both *sado* fanatics. My house is still full of tea bowls and other bits and pieces of tea ceremony stuff... very expensive, and I don't know what to do with it all, actually...."

Penelope, who knew many tea fanatics, told him she understood all too well.

"I was particularly interested in the fact that at one point or other they had women *iemoto*. Do you know anything about that?" she asked. "It just struck me as kind of odd...."

"Oh... that's right, they did... I think it was, when was it, in the mid-nineteenth century. Suiko and.... another one....."

"Saya. 1830's," Penelope volunteered.

Shimada-san nodded.

"Yes, that's the one. Takahashi Saya. Fascinating lady. She was the first one. You know she bumped off her husband? So the story goes anyway."

"Is that so… no, I didn't know that," said Penelope

Shimada-san crossed his arms and sat back in his seat.

"She was a very upper-class lady from a *daimyo* family that had kind of fallen on hard times. A branch of the Date family, relatives of the ruling Tokugawa *shoguns* of the Edo Period. Anyway, in those days, marrying into a tea school was a decided step down the ladder, at least from where she came from. Anyway, she was his second wife, and he already had an heir, who was very young at the time, and her own child was not going to fit into the line of succession as a result."

Shimada-san leaned forward and whispered,

"Anyway, one night on his way home from the tea houses, I mean the red light area that her husband was so fond of visiting, he had an 'accident.' They found his body floating under a bridge in the Sumida River the next day. And then she took over. No one dared go against her, after all, she was n*obi*lity basically, and that counted for a lot back then. And she stayed in charge for nearly twenty years and in the process made sure her own son succeeded her, rather than the elder half-brother. She was quite… formidable, by all accounts. I have a picture of her at my house somewhere if you ever want to see it."

Penelope was engrossed, and she liked the way Shimada-san had of bringing history to life like this. When he spoke of these long-dead people, it seemed that he had known them personally.

"That's amazing. Yes, I would love to see her. Maybe another time. What about the other one?"

Shimada-san closed his eyes.

"Suiko. Yes, maybe the 1870s?"

175

"Yes, that's right. She had the job maybe about five or ten years."

Shimada-san nodded.

"Yes... she was a bit less interesting. Also from a good family, like Saya, but without the nasty habits. Her husband also died, I think of consumption. It was one of the number one killers back then, not only in Japan but also in Europe, as you probably know. Anyway, they had several children, but the oldest son was pretty young at the time of the husband's death, so she took over until he was old enough to do the job. It was a fairly normal arrangement; after all, Saya had already blazed a trail for her, and people were used to the idea. Suiko always made it clear she would hand over the job as soon as the boy was old enough. I think that boy was the great-grandfather of the current one who died the other day...."

"So, no foul play?" asked Penelope.

"No, not that I know of," said Shimada-san. "Would you like another coffee? I come here pretty often. They know me by now, I think....."

He gestured around at the old cafe, which was one of those old traditional ones that you still found in Japan, with big mirrors on the wall and low tables with upholstered furniture and where the coffee was usually made by an old connoisseur behind the counter and took about twenty minutes before it had carefully dripped and was ready.

"It's a lovely old place, isn't it?" said Penelope.

Shimada-san nodded and adjusted his cuffs.

"I think I first came here as a boy actually... with my father. It's still going... somehow. Tell me, though..." he leaned forward again. "Is it true the family has a tea bowl... by Sen no Rikyu?"

Penelope nodded.

"It would seem so. Momoko, who will be the next *iemoto*, showed me a picture. The father had it verified and everything in Osaka."

Shimada-san let out a low whistle.

"I should very much like to see such a thing. I've seen a few in museums... but to own such a thing... that's really something," he said.

Penelope could feel his palpable enthusiasm and, at the same time, what the past meant to him.

"Yes, well, you may have the chance. She's going to have an *ochakai* soon. That was also her father's plan, only he died before he could do it. They are going to exhibit it at the event. I will make sure you get a ticket," she said with a smile.

Shimada-san thanked her and ordered two more cups of strong coffee and some roll cake, which was one of the specialties of the old cafe.

"You know, it's interesting that they have such a tea bowl in more ways than one," he said as he took some cake and touched his mouth with his handkerchief, which he once again arranged neatly on the table.

"How so," said Penelope.

Shimada-san smiled knowingly.

"Because she is Rikyu's descendent. Didn't she tell you that? Both her and her late brother, of course."

Penelope's eyes widened.

"Seriously? I had no idea. She has never mentioned *that* to me. Or anyone I know..." she exclaimed, thinking that

Fujimoto-san would surely have told her that if she had known about it.

"But how? I didn't know that the Takahashi family were descended from Rikyu. I thought that was the Sen family at the big Urasenke School and those people. If the Takahashi's were descended from Rikyu, it seems strange to me they wouldn't advertise the fact," said Penelope.

Shimada-san shook his head.

"They aren't. It's not the Takahashi family. It's her mother's family. The Akigawa family. And they actually have a better claim than even the other tea schools. Her mother Sachiko comes from an old Sakai family that are descended from Doan, Rikyu's eldest son. For some reason back then, it was a younger son by the second wife that came to be known as the next in line after his father's death, and that is where the big tea schools claim their lineage from. And that's all perfectly correct," he said.

"But Takahashi Momoko, she is the real deal, a direct descendent of Rikyu's eldest son. So her late mother and her are much more tea 'royalty' if you'll pardon the term, than the Takahashi clan. They have no connection to the Rikyu line at all. They are kind of, you know, 'new money' as the British say, compared to Momoko's family. That's no doubt why he wanted her as a wife, though by all accounts it was a love match," said Shimada-san.

"I didn't know the Akigawa family were that involved with tea. I mean, they didn't have a school or anything."

Shimada-san shook his head.

"No, they didn't. After the death of Doan, his heirs became prominent merchants in the city of Sakai, near Osaka, where the Sen family came from. They were always supporters of the tea ceremony and prominent collectors of tea artifacts. The family branched out in different ways, and some of them became very wealthy. So when old Takahashi got his claws into Sachiko, not only did he get the money, but he also got a connection to the Rikyu lineage. He seems to have been pretty vain, and maybe he didn't want it known that his wife's family was richer and more connected to tea than his. So maybe that's why they chose to keep it quiet. I'm not sure… but that would be my idea. I spoke to his late wife when I was writing my book, and she confirmed it was true, but she also didn't seem to want to make a big deal of it, so I didn't write about it. I always thought she was a true lady…" he said.

"But I wouldn't imagine Momoko *iemoto* will keep it quiet for long, not if she is going to show off her ancestor's very own creation…."

Penelope sat back in her seat in surprise, her mind racing over the implications of what she had just learned.

"No, you're right, Shimada-san. I wouldn't imagine she would…" she said thoughtfully.

They talked for a while longer, and then the elderly gentleman said he must be going, as he had promised to look after one of his grandchildren that afternoon.

"I hope you don't mind, but I bought you a copy of my book; I had a spare one lying around, just in case you needed it in the future for your research… I signed it for you…." he showed her his inscription on the title page.

Penelope thanked him profusely for his time and promised to meet him again soon at the *ochakai* and that she would arrange tickets for him.

As she walked through the little winding streets, she would find that she had another surprise waiting for her at home.

========================

"She's been arrested," said Fei.

Penelope threw her bag on the table and sat down in her usual old wicker chair next to her friend, who had just come from the police station where she had been on the morning shift at the mortuary.

"Who's been arrested?" said Penelope.

"Haruko-san, of course. They've just brought her down to the station. She's being detained for questioning. I'm pretty sure they intend to charge her though, you know that lot..." she said grimly. "They don't usually put you in cuffs if they don't mean it."

Penelope was stunned. "Why? What have they found?"

Fei lit up her pipe and blew her usual stream of smoke into the garden.

"I only got about five minutes with Yamashita-san, they were just about to start the interrogation, so I dunno all the details, but they found out that she was the one who had bought the cyanide recently."

"Wow. They traced it? To her?" asked Penelope.

"Yep. Well, I presume so, anyway. They couldn't find any record of it on her computer, but they traced it to the shop where apparently she picked it up and paid cash just a month ago. They have video footage from the shop. So I would say the next thing they will do is ransack the house until they find the rest; that's presuming she doesn't tell them where it is, or more likely that she got rid of it somewhere. According to what I hear, she bought enough to poison ten husbands, let alone one."

Fei, who loved a good crime drama, was clearly in her element this afternoon.

"Well, that was always the question, you know, where did the cyanide come from? There was no sign that the old boy ever bought it or got someone else to buy it. Apart from the traces in the bowl, they only found it in the tea caddy that was used, there was enough in there to poison a rhinoceros. But the rest of it… that seemed to be gone."

Penelope nodded. "Yes, I always wondered about that too. There was no need to put it in the tea caddy and mix it with the tea unless you were trying to conceal it. Which means it couldn't have been suicide. I mean, why do that? Why not just put it in the bowl itself?"

"Of course," she continued, "the other way to look at that is that he was a tea master, and that's not how you make tea. Mixing it into the tea in the container would be much more aesthetically pleasing, and then putting a few scoops in the bowl in the normal manner."

Fei shook her head and wagged the long stem of her pipe at her friend.

"That's overthinking it, I reckon. If the poison was in the tea caddy, which it was, it is most likely done to conceal it.

The bitterness of the tea would mask the taste whichever way you did it, but it's much more likely someone else put it in there and he didn't know about it."

Penelope nodded. She had to admit that Fei had logic on her side.

"But what about motive?" she asked. "Why would she want to bump off her husband just when he has this priceless artifact and a deal on the table to sell the school? And don't forget, she was the one who did the negotiating, by all accounts, and at his direction. That doesn't make much sense."

Fei gave her an arch look.

"Well, apart from the fact that hubby was a perfect pig of a human being, there might also be the fact that she was bonking the Inamoto heir, with whom she was doing the negotiating..." said Fei, showing off her advanced knowledge of London slang once again.

"Possibly. Are they going to talk to Inamoto? Maybe he was in on it too, do you think?" asked Penelope.

Fei nodded.

"Now that you mention it, I'm sure that's crossed Yamashita-san's mind."

They were both quiet for a moment, contemplating these new developments and staring out at the clouds gathering outside.

Finally, Penelope broke the silence.

"You know what this means too, don't you."

Fei looked at her inquiringly.

"If she knocked off Issei too, to get his share of the school... was Momoko going to be next? Momoko has totally scuppered the sale now and in public.... And I saw how that idea went down with Haruko firsthand. She looked furious," said Penelope thoughtfully.

"Very true," she said quietly. "Young Momoko-san may have dodged a bullet there...."

Chapter 17

The Bamboo Temple

Sometimes, when Penelope wanted to think, she would make the journey to Hokokuji, a small but quite famous temple known by everyone as Take-dera, or the Bamboo Temple.

It was a well-known tourist destination, so the best time to go there was early in the morning or in the afternoon around closing time, in order to miss the crowds. On sunny days the extensive bamboo forest surrounding the temple was well-loved, especially among photographers, for the way the sunlight shone fell through the canopy of leaves, and in the rainy season when the intense green of the bamboo shone in the mist and rain and filled the mind with the image of water and the sound of the leaves moving in the breeze.

The temple was founded in the fourteenth century and was an important Rinzai Zen training monastery, and originally the bamboo grove had been set aside as a place for the monks to meditate in peace, and this was what Penelope also found whenever she went there, that the atmosphere enabled her to empty her mind and see whatever problems she had with a clarity she often did not find at home.

Unable to sleep, she had risen earlier than usual and gone for a short walk around her neighborhood, enjoying the cool of the morning, and then she had thought about Hokokuji, and how long it had been since she had been there. Seeing a passing taxi and on a whim of the moment, she had found her hand in the air and herself hopping inside for the short ride to her destination. About ten minutes later, she was walking down the quiet little lane from the main road that led to the entrance to the temple with its elegant gateway, overhung by the bright green of its maples, sparkling in the morning sun.

It felt good to do something spontaneous for once, and to her pleasure, she found that she was one of only a few visitors this morning. As she had been here many times before, she walked past the main hall to the rear of the temple and took the little flag-stoned path that led into the bamboo forest, where she found herself alone with just the trees and her thoughts for company.

The temple had gone through many changes in its long history, but it was not hard to see the attraction of this quiet place for anyone who came seeking a place of refuge from the world outside. It must have been seen as such right from the very beginning, as the temple was founded during one of the most turbulent moments in the country's history, when powerful warlords had fought almost ceaseless wars in their pursuit of power. Even the founder of the temple, the grandfather of a future *shogun*, had been forced by the internecine strife to commit ritual suicide, and his remains were buried, it was said, in a cave here in the bamboo grove.

That morning Penelope had other things on her mind besides history, however.

She wandered along the path until she came to a little rest area in the middle of the grove which served macha green tea and sweets, and took advantage of the lack of customers at that time to enjoy a bowl of tea and a small sweet, and to take a moment to sit on the little bench that overlooked the forest.

The tea was hot and perfectly whisked to a nice froth, and she ate the sweet that came with it slowly and allowed it to cool for a moment before holding the bowl in both hands and allowing the soft bitterness to lie on her tongue. For that moment, she focused her mind only on the taste of the tea and nothing else, allowing herself the pleasure of a moment of complete absorption in the present. The highly caffeinated tea flooded her senses and refreshed her almost instantly, and as she returned to the world around her, she turned her thoughts once more to the Takahashi situation, which had been troubling her now for days, especially since Haruko's arrest and incarceration in the Kamakura police station, where even now her interrogation was continuing at the hand of her friend Chief Inspector Yamashita and his subordinates.

Things had not been going well for Haruko, yet even with the new evidence that had been discovered she had steadfastly maintained her innocence. Most seriously, there had been a significant find at the house, and more specifically in her own room.

After her arrest, the police had obtained a search warrant for the Takahashi estate and had, in search of Haruko's bedroom, located a clear jar containing a white powder hidden in a shoebox in her closet. The contents had been quickly tested and identified as cyanide, and moreover, a poison of the same toxicity and type as had been ingested by her late husband, whose death had been immediately re-categorized as having occurred due to 'unknown circumstances' rather than the original verdict of suicide.

Penelope sat with her tea and enjoyed the peace of the forest and the feel of the warm bowl in her hand as she turned these events over in her mind.

There were so many things about this case that troubled her, things which she did not have answers to, and questions that continued to swirl in her mind. Fei had kept her informed of the progress of the interrogation, which was not making much progress to tell the truth, and of the recent findings the police had made in building their case against Haruko.

One of the most important, and also most worryingly inconclusive, was the discovery of a surveillance tape taken at a convenience store in nearby Zushi, a seaside resort very close to Kamakura that was popular with boat owners and the many wealthy folk who owned summer houses in the area.

This tape showed a woman wearing jeans and a black sports shirt entering the store and picking up a box containing what was thought to be the poison used to kill the *iemoto*.

It was extremely common for people to pick up things they had ordered at their local convenience store, especially if it was not something they wanted left in their post box or on their doorstep if they were at work or some other place, so there was nothing unusual in this. The problem was, however, that because the woman, if it was a woman, was impossible to identify considering that she (or he) was also wearing a baseball cap pulled down low over a pair of dark sunglasses and a facemask. The person wore no identifiable rings or jewelry and had no other distinguishing features. There was only the camera over the counter to look at, and there were no cameras outside the store to provide any more information. So whereas it *could* be Haruko, it also could be literally anyone.

The goods had been ordered online from an anonymous account in the name of H. Takahashi, using a computer at one of the local libraries in Kamakura, and paid for in cash. Once again, there was no way to confirm this at the library, which did not have any working cameras near their free internet service area, if indeed the person using the computer had been Haruko.

A final point of confusion was the jar used to contain the cyanide that had been found in her room. The cyanide was sold in a black plastic container with a white screw top lid. However, the jar found hidden in Haruko's room was an old jar that had once contained a common type of pasta sauce sold at supermarkets across the country. The question, of course, was, why would she have put the remains of the cyanide in a different jar, which had her fingerprints all over it, and where was the original container?

On being shown the jar, Haruko had maintained that she had never seen it before in her life, and on being told it bore her fingerprints, had maintained that the jar was one of many that you could find in the kitchen and that she had made pasta using that same type of jar many times in the past. True, she could have been trying to disguise the jar's contents, so why not just throw the rest of the cyanide away? Why not just flush it down the toilet? Why keep the evidence of a crime in her own closet?

Penelope had known Haruko for many years by this point, and one thing she knew was that Haruko was no fool. She may have hated her husband, but she was not stupid enough to poison the man and then leave the evidence in her room. And as a former chemist and researcher, she could also have easily made some highly toxic substance herself rather than expose herself to the risk of using the internet and a convenience store with cameras to buy something commercially.

The police, however, seemed convinced that not only had she done all of these inexplicable things to incriminate herself for the death of her husband, but that her stepson's death also could also be laid at her door owing to the fact that she had been the one to order the deadly sesame sweets.

However, once again, the trail that led to her involvement in Issei's death was less than clear.

Haruko maintained that she had no idea that they were hosting any tea gathering that day, that she had never been informed about this by Momoko and had never spoken to Issei about any such thing. Also, because Issei rarely ate *wagashi*, the school had been ordering the same sweet for years, knowing full well that Issei was completely aware of the danger, which had been drummed into him since childhood. And even if he had not been aware of these particular sweets, he would have known quite well to question the safety of eating them based on his knowledge that tea sweets often contained sesame.

He hadn't done this, so presumably Haruko had told him the sweets he was going to eat that day were safe. But once again, when had she done this? Haruko had left the house in the early morning to visit Inamoto in Ibaraki, a long distance away to the north of Tokyo. There was no evidence she had seen Issei to tell him this dangerous lie before she left. Issei was well-known never to get up before 11 am, as he had indeed done that day as was attested by the cook, who had made him his morning coffee.

And so the uncertainty continued to swirl around Haruko. At this point the police were unwilling to charge her on such circumstantial evidence without a clear motive, and were pinning their hopes on a confession which it seemed increasingly unlikely they would get.

Penelope finished her tea and discovered she was no longer alone in the little rest area, as a large group of tourists had just arrived from somewhere and were noisily ordering their refreshments, so she decided that this might be a good time to leave. She paid her bill and wandered further up the path to where it forked, and where she found a row of grave markers next to a small stupa that presumably marked the burial place of several ancient monks.

She paused here and looked at the figures of the monks that had been carved into the little stone markers and marveled at how life-like the faces were, even after all this time and all the weather that had slowly etched itself on the stone.

It was like a snapshot of their lives in a way. Not like so many effigies you found in English and European churches, their eyes closed and their hands clasped in prayer upon their chests.

They looked happy, she thought. Calm and happy and serene, like their lives had been fulfilled in this place. Like they were talking to you and had something profound to say if you would listen. Almost as if they wanted to reach out with their hands and smiling faces and bless you somehow.

She envied them that serenity, that effortless confidence in their own peacefulness.

For her, no matter how drawn she was to Zen Buddhism and meditation, and no matter how many years she had studied at Engakuji with her friend and mentor Dokan, she knew herself as well. Her mind was a hive of ideas that would simply not stop moving, that could not stop buzzing with possibilities and seeking the next thing. Once she was handed a puzzle, or any task, whether it was a research topic or a book project or something like this Takahashi thing, there was no way she could let it go, no way she could move on until she had finished it and tied up every loose end to her own satisfaction.

It was just impossible for her. And sometimes, like now, it bothered her.

She knelt down and ran her hand over one of the monk's faces and felt the rough stone under her fingers.

"*I will never be like you,*" she thought sadly.

For the next half hour or so, she drifted along the little pathways around the bamboo forest in different directions and eventually found herself back at the main gate, where yet another group of tourists let by their flag-waving guide was heading towards her.

She decided it was time to finish her impromptu excursion and to go home and get on with her work. But she was glad she had listened to her instincts and taken this little trip, and she quietly resolved that she would do this kind of thing more often. After all, she was retired, could do what she wanted, and didn't need to spend all her days cooped up writing. There were other things in life, she reflected.

The tour group approached, and she heard the murmur of their voices trailing away up the path as she headed in the other direction. Some of the tourists were listening to information on headphones, which struck her as odd. Why didn't they just listen to the guide? Why would they prefer to listen to a recording? Maybe they just didn't understand their guide, perhaps that was it. It did look strange to see people outside in the fresh air with headphones on. Maybe that's how people do things on tours these days, she thought.

She walked back to the main road and stood waiting at the stop for the bus back to Kamakura station. Would it be quicker to walk? It probably only took about twenty minutes.

There was no bus in sight and no timetable, so she turned and started up the road towards the town center.

And then it hit her.

The idea came with such force that she caught herself swaying slightly as she walked. There was a little low wall behind the bus stop, and she took a seat and involuntarily put her hand to her mouth like she was in shock.

Sometimes, when a long-sought answer finally occurred to her, she remembered being with her father on the Windrush River near Oxford, where he had attempted to teach her what he called the 'art' of fly fishing. During those long and lovely afternoons they spent together, standing in the shallow river in their waders or fishing from the banks, she would go through the same feelings over and over. A fish would bite the lure, the line would go taught, and your heart would jump in excitement, but then that feeling was almost instantly replaced by the fear that at any moment if you made any false move, it would just slip off the line and disappear and then be gone forever.

She found that ideas, especially epiphanies like this, were the same. They were gone no sooner than they flashed into your mind, searing across the darkness like a comet in the night sky and vanishing.

That was exactly what this moment felt like, and she was paralyzed by the sudden fear that it, too, was going to vanish like smoke.

She sat on the old stone wall and closed her eyes and pictured it, holding it in her mind and locking down the details of the image that had suddenly come to her.

There were two people, and they were talking in a library.

Now she had it.

"*Oh… you're so clever,*" she thought.

And yet the compliment was not addressed to herself.

"*Clever, clever, clever.*"

==================

She had always found that if she wrote down her ideas, she was able to see them clearly, so the first thing she did when she went home was to go to her study, where she spent the next three hours with pen and paper and her computer going over and over her solution, turning it in her hand like a precious jewel, looking at it from different directions and checking for flaws.

As an academic, this was always the way she had worked, first coming up with an idea, then assembling the data to support or disprove it, then putting the whole thing together like a giant jigsaw puzzle until she could see it like a chain of facts, each link connected to the one before it and the one after it, unbroken and leading to a conclusion.

No matter what she did with her thesis though, and no matter how many questions she asked of it, the answer was the same.

It was possible.

And if it was possible, then all she had to do was to find a way to prove it.

"*Easier said than done though,*" she thought to herself. But she knew she had a way, yet only if she were as clever as the person who had laid out the problem in the first place.

Even more difficult was that she would have to find a way to convince Fei and then Chief Inspector Yamashita to give her the chance to do it.

Would they take that chance on her?

There was only one way to find out, and she dreaded having to do it.

She picked up her phone and dialed Fei, who she knew was not at work today, and a half hour later she was sitting in her living room.

"So, what's the big emergency?" asked Fei as she dropped into her chair and rummaged in her bag for her pipe and tobacco.

Penelope poured them both a glass of wine.

"I need you to listen to a story and not interrupt. Can you do that?" she said, passing her the glass.

Fei raised an eyebrow. "Of course. You know I love a good story," she said, and smiled at her old friend.

"Good. Because you are going to love this one."

Chapter 18

J'accuse

The next morning, after a day of hurried arrangements, two police cars arrived at the Takahashi estate.

In the first car, driven by a detective sergeant, were Chief Inspector Yamashita and Haruko Takahashi, whose handcuffs had been removed for the occasion.

Their excursion this morning had caused some consternation among the police investigating the crime, as suspects under interrogation were usually detained in a cell and not allowed to leave the station under almost any circumstances except to see the prosecutor to discuss their case. However, the Chief Inspector had argued that it was necessary to further the investigation that she accompany him to attend the appointment they had arranged this morning.

Yamashita had also acceded to Penelope's request for Eriko to be present and had arranged for her to be driven to the estate in the same unmarked car he had arranged for Penelope and Fei.

When they arrived, Momoko met them at the front door with a smile, even though it was clear she was surprised to see not only Haruko standing next to a uniformed police officer but also Eriko, the maid she had so peremptorily fired just a few weeks before.

"Well, it's nice to see you all again," she said. "Would you like to come in?"

Momoko was wearing an elegant white one-piece dress with a long lapis necklace and had her beautiful long hair loose and falling to her waist.

"Do you think it would be possible to use the main tea house? I think we should discuss a few things about tea, and it would be great if you could help us…." asked Yamashita pleasantly.

"The tea house? Oh, I'm sorry, we haven't cleaned that recently. I… er…wouldn't you rather sit in the library?" said Momoko, looking slightly confused.

"No, actually, the tea house would be the best place. Please don't worry about the cleaning. I should have mentioned it to you before we came."

Momoko shrugged.

"OK, sure. Please forgive the mess, however. It really should be dusted before we have guests in there. These old buildings are terrible for dust…" she said.

She led the way around the side of the house through the gardens, and they arrived at the main tea house, where Momoko unlocked the door and gestured for them to go in.

One by one, they all crouched and entered the old room through the low *nijiriguchi* doorway, and Momoko gave them all some navy-blue *zabuton* cushions to sit on.

There were six of them in the room now, Momoko, Penelope, Fei, Eriko, Chief Inspector Yamashita and

Haruko, while the uniformed officer remained outside at Yamashita's request. They sat in a small half circle on the tatami mat floor, all in the somewhat uncomfortable yet traditional *seiza* style with their legs folded under them, which even Yamashita and Fei, who were not as used to it as the tea practitioners, managed to assume.

Penelope prepared the materials she was going to use, and from her rucksack she produced a laptop, which she opened and put on the floor so that they could all see it, which caused several of them to stare at her in bemusement.

Haruko, however, had clearly reached her limit that morning of not knowing what was about to happen.

"Look, nobody has had the courtesy to tell me what all this is about," said Haruko in a firm tone. "You've just dragged me out of the police station, without my lawyer present and brought me here. I want an explanation, please, and I want it now if you would be so kind."

Yamashita smiled at her.

"That's exactly what you are going to get, Takahashi-san. An explanation. After we have finished here today, I would be interested to hear anything you have to say, or if there is any way you have been unfairly treated. Until then, please answer any questions you are asked. Could you kindly agree to that?" he said with a polite smile.

Haruko looked more surprised than affronted, but nodded her assent while all the time glaring at Momoko, who avoided her eyes.

Yamashita cleared his throat.

"Very well. Penny-*sensei*, you may begin," he said.

All eyes turned on Penelope with some surprise, as most of them thought they were gathered to listen to the chief inspector.

Penelope gave them all a slight bow and smiled.

"I'm sorry to have inconvenienced all of you by asking you to come today. I know you are all busy with other things…" she said, making the usual and most common of Japanese style beginnings. "But if you could just bear with me a while, hopefully, things will become clear," she said.

"Of course," said Momoko politely, no doubt thinking she should say something as she was the host and they were sitting in her tea house.

"Please go ahead, Penny-*sensei*."

Penny bowed her head again to acknowledge her remark.

"Thank you, Momoko-san," she said.

There was a short silence while she seemed to gather her thoughts before she spoke again.

"Let's start at the beginning, with a tea bowl made by Sen no Rikyu…" she began. "Your father must have been so delighted when that was found… wasn't he?" Penelope asked Momoko brightly.

Momoko nodded and smiled.

Yes, we were all delighted. I'm sorry… it's not here at the moment to show you. He put it in the bank…" she said.

"But that must have been quite a moment for him. And especially for you and your brother, wouldn't that be correct?"

Momoko smiled. "Yes, of course. We were all happy, like I said."

"But you, and maybe Issei too… you must have been particularly moved… to have something in your hands

199

made by your own ancestor. Even your father never knew that feeling, right?"

Momoko blushed and shook her head.

Penelope cocked her head inquiringly at her. "Well, you and Issei *are* Rikyu's direct ancestors, I am right about that, aren't I? On your mother's side?"

Momoko looked up and gave a nervous smile. "Yes, that's true. My mother told us about it before she passed away. I didn't think anyone but us knew about it…."

Penelope nodded. "Would I be right in saying that your father also didn't want it to be that well-known? Maybe because your own heritage was much more… elite? Would that be the right word?"

Momoko shrugged noncommittally and shuffled a little on her cushion.

"Well, he was a proud man. And proud of the Takahashi name too. Actually, many people must be descended from Sen no Rikyu in Japan. We are not the only ones," Momoko said modestly.

"That's true," said Haruko. "He didn't like people talking about it. He wanted everyone to focus on his own line… that was the most important thing to him."

"But surely, it would have been an advantage to the school to have a future *iemoto*; you know I am talking about Issei here, who was a direct ancestor of Rikyu? That would put you on the same level as the major schools, would it not?" asked Penelope.

"Perhaps," said Haruko. "But he had decided to sell. In that case, it would have seemed even more of a betrayal if that information had become public."

"I understand," said Penelope. "Well, it looks like everything has worked out well then, as the school will not be sold, and it will now be led by a new *iemoto*, who is indeed a direct descendant of the master himself. Isn't that a wonderful thing?" she said.

Momoko blushed again and smiled at Penelope and the others.

"I'm going to do my best," she said and looked modestly at the floor.

Penelope nodded. "I know you will, my dear. I know you will. I have known you since you were very young... you were born to do this, I think," she smiled.

"Thank you, Penny-*sensei*. You and Fujimoto-san have always been my friends, I know that."

"Yes, we have," said Penelope. "Which is why I have been so worried about you, and have been trying to understand why all of this happened. First, your father. Then your brother... it's been truly awful."

Momoko nodded and brushed away a tear.

"You must have been shocked by his decision to sell the school, right? When did you first find out about it?" asked Penelope.

Momoko sat up straight.

"Find out? I don't know. A few months ago. Ask her... she was the one who talked him into it," she said, nodding towards Haruko but not looking at her directly.

"A few months ago... so that's around May? Or June?"

"May," said Haruko. "Right before he found the bowl. He thought it would add immeasurably to the sale and that we could drive a better bargain with the Inamoto family. And he was right. They increased their offer immediately," she said.

"By how much?" asked Penelope.

Haruko paused. "They immediately offered another fifty million yen if we would add the bowl to the sale of the school. I think we could have got more, actually. Anyway, with the sale of the school and the bowl, we would have been able to clear all our debts and have plenty left over to live. And the school would have continued, anyway. It would just be run by another tea family. That kind of thing used to happen all the time in the old days."

"Maybe, but not by selling. It would have been because there was no male heir to inherit the *iemoto* title, right?" said Penelope.

Haruko looked down at the floor.

"Possibly."

Momoko sneered.

"Not possibly. Never. But our school has a history of female *iemoto*. I will be the third actually," she said.

"Yes. That is exactly how I thought you would feel, Momoko-san. Tea should never be about money, should it?" asked Penelope politely.

"Of course not. It's never about money. It is an art. An art which is a tradition of this house," she looked about the room, her eyes shining proudly.

There was a long silence in the room, and Penelope stared at Momoko unblinkingly.

"And so, you had to stop the sale, didn't you?" she said quietly.

Momoko, beginning to sense that she had said too much, turned her head quickly towards Penelope.

"It was Papa's decision. Of course, Haruko probably talked him into it. But it was his decision. There was nothing I could do about it. Except tell him it was wrong. And I did that. I told all of you that it was wrong."

She glared again at Haruko.

Fei and Eriko, listening quietly, shifted awkwardly on their cushions, but the Chief Inspector sat unmoving with the same unreadable smile on his lips.

Penelope looked carefully at Momoko.

"They wouldn't listen to you, would they? They also could not understand you, Momoko-san. That losing the school would mean far more to you than even your father…."

Momoko nodded furiously. "That's right. They couldn't. They didn't even give it a thought. All they wanted… was the *money*!" She spat the word in Haruko's face, who sat throughout with a dignified silence and an unchanging expression.

Penelope waited a moment to give Momoko a chance to regain her calm.

"So… you acted," she said.

Momoko stared at her with a confused expression.

"What do you mean… acted? I didn't do anything. There was nothing I could do… I told you."

Penelope smiled.

"Do I need to explain what happened then?" she asked.

There was silence for a moment, and Momoko stared around the room as if looking for support, and when it was not forthcoming, she turned quietly to Penelope.

"I'm sorry, I don't understand…" she said.

Penelope sighed.

"OK, if that's your wish then, I will explain. So please listen, Momoko-san, and if I have got anything wrong, you can tell me at the end. Is that OK?"

"Of course. Go ahead, Penny-*sensei*. But I don't really know…" she began.

Penelope smiled at her like she was a small child.

"The first thing to understand, is that when you killed your father that night, you were not alone. Issei helped you."

At that moment, the color completely left Momoko's face. She stared at Penelope, but said nothing.

"You planned it very well, over the course of at least a month. I will get to that a little later because that was done extremely cleverly. But let's just talk about the night he died first," she said calmly.

"By this stage, you had already talked Issei into helping you, no doubt making the case that if your father sold the school, then he would be stealing his heritage, taking away his title, and worst of all, your father and Haruko would be getting all the money to spend as they liked, potentially leaving poor Issei and you with nothing."

"I think, for Issei, that must have been a very strong argument indeed to help you get your father… out of the picture, so to speak. Especially given his rather extravagant tastes…."

Momoko shook her head. "It wasn't like that," she hissed.

Penelope ignored her.

"And so, Momoko-san, that night after dinner, you asked your father for a special favor. Would he allow you to make tea for him, maybe for the last time ever, using the bowl made by your own ancestor, the very founder of the tea ceremony himself…Sen no Rikyu."

Momoko shook her head again.

"And, of course, what father would say no to that? Issei said he also wanted to participate; it would be a private moment, just a father and his children… alone with all that history. It has a kind of…poignancy about it, don't you think?"

Momoko glared at her. "You are just making this up. It never happened like that. I thought you were my friend, Penny-*sensei*…."

Penelope smiled. "I am your friend, Momoko-san. But let me continue. OK?"

Momoko looked away and addressed the wall.

"Sure. Whatever," she sneered.

After a brief pause, Penelope continued her explanation.

"The three of you went to the tea house that evening after dinner. Father, son, and daughter…. And I think you had everything ready, didn't you? All prepared, the water boiling, the equipment laid out. The sweets. Everything waiting. And then you asked your father for the bowl, which he had ready for the *ochakai* the next day. It was never in the bank; that never made sense. I think he wanted it near him, and he didn't want to have to be going to the bank on the day of the event. He had it here, in this room. Probably still sitting in its original box."

"And so… he gave it to you, and for the first time ever, you made tea using Rikyu's own creation. You, his ancestor. That must have been a moment for you, I think…."

Momoko said nothing and continued to look away.

"And then you scooped the tea, which you had mixed with the poison, into the bowl, and added the water, and whisked it... And then, because your father was the chief guest, you gave it to him to drink first."

"And all the time, Issei was sitting next to your father, watching his sister make the tea. He sat beside him and watched as he raised the bowl and drank... You both just watched him. You watched as his body started to convulse; you watched him as he lay writhing in agony on the floor... You watched him as he lay dying."

"And you did nothing. Nothing at all...."

Penelope paused and let her words sink into her.

"I wonder if you even spoke to him, even just to say goodbye...."

Momoko's shoulders began to shudder, but then she controlled herself and continued to look away.

Penelope paused for a moment, watching her, and then she continued.

"And then you calmly tidied up the room. You replaced the bowl with another bowl, which you had also made a bowl of poisoned tea in, and you dropped that on the floor next to your father's body. Of course, you would never leave the real bowl lying on the floor, would you? That's far too valuable to you. And after you did all this, the pair of you left the room and went back to the house and watched television for an hour."

Momoko turned round and glared at her.

"That is a complete lie."

She looked angrily at Yamashita, who had not moved a muscle in all the time Penelope had been speaking. "It's complete rubbish. I did no such thing. Neither did Issei. We had dinner. We talked. We watched TV. We went nowhere near this tea house. We had nothing to do with Papa's death. Nothing!!" she shouted at him.

Momoko jumped to her feet and headed toward the door.

"Takahashi-san," said the inspector.

"What? I'm not going to sit here and listen to …."

"You will sit down," the Chief Inspector said quietly but with such authority that Momoko stopped in her tracks.

"You will not leave this room until we have finished. If you attempt to do so, I will ask that officer outside to take you to the police station in handcuffs. Do you understand me?"

Momoko meekly returned to her cushion and resumed her seat, but now her face was ashen, and her hands visibly trembled.

"Very well," she said. "Let's get this over with."

"I agree," said Penelope calmly. "Let's do that."

"Up till this point," she continued, "I have explained *what* you did that night. Now I will tell you *how* you almost got away with it. And also, I'm going to show you how you *haven't.*"

Chapter 19

Who's Afraid of Virginia Woolf?

"Let's start with the poison. That seems the best place to begin, as that was what you managed to procure back in May after your father announced he was going to sell the school," Penelope began.

"It would seem clear that from the very beginning, you intended to frame Haruko for your father's death. So you started by creating a fake mail account in her name and ordering the poison using this. You then arranged to pick it up and paid in cash at a small convenience store located some distance away, where you dressed in some of Haruko's clothes and also borrowed a pair of her sunglasses. Haruko doesn't drive, so she would never have missed it, but she has a driving license in her purse, so you took this with you so you could use it as ID when you picked up the goods."

"Nonsense. I've done no such thing," said Momoko flatly.

"Really? Maybe you are not aware, but it's going to be fairly simple to compare your fingerprints to the partial one that Chief Inspector Yamashita tells me we have on her license. But let's go on for now," said Penelope.

Momoko eye's opened slightly at this, but she made no other response.

"You then returned home, where you washed her clothes and put them back in her wardrobe so that there was no DNA trace on them. If there was, you could always say it came from when you helped with the laundry or some other lie in any case," said Penelope.

"You did have one other problem, though: Haruko's fingerprints were not on the poison container, only yours. How were you going to arrange this? In the end, you made use of a pasta sauce container that Haruko had put out with some other glass items for the rubbish, and you then poured the rest of the cyanide into this. Now you have a container full of cyanide with Haruko's prints on it, and you later planted this in her bedroom."

"There was one point, though, which was rather risky for you, I think. You seem to have ignored the question of why Haruko would put the cyanide into the other jar if she were just going to keep it in her bedroom, where it could be easily found. That makes no sense at all, but that didn't occur to you, it seems. It certainly made the police pay attention, though..." she said, glancing at Yamashita san, who gave a brief but non-committal nod.

"Anything to say yet?"

Penelope paused and waited to see if Momoko would reply, but there was no response from her, and she continued to look at the floor in silence.

"OK, let's go on. All you had to do then was to lure your father into this room and kill him, as I have already described. By the way...." Penelope smiled slightly. "Do you know how I know that Issei was with you?"

Momoko looked at her with an air of disinterest and raised one eyebrow.

"Because Issei, as everyone in the family knew, did not just suffer from a severe allergy to sesame. He also had a small mental issue, well, don't we all, but in his case, it is called OCD, or Obsessive-Compulsive Disorder. Eriko told me how incredibly tidy everything was, how all the clothes were color-coded in the wardrobe, and how all his books were alphabetically ordered by category on their shelves. How all the food had to be just so…."

Penelope paused.

"Of course, you were used to him. But that's how we know your brother was with you… when you poisoned your father."

Momoko looked away again.

"Because Issei, who cannot tolerate disorder of any kind… could not stop himself from turning out the light when he left the tea house…."

Penelope looked up and saw Fei staring at her with unrestrained admiration and smiled at her warmly as if to say, "Don't worry, I forgive you for not understanding."

Momoko, however, looked up at her and coughed.

"So, Penny-*sensei*, how do you know it was not Issei who did all this then? And by the way, anyone could have turned out that light…" she smiled haughtily.

"Perhaps," said Penelope. "But we do know *you* were there. And we know you were not in the house talking with Issei in the library."

Momoko glared at her.

"That's a lie. We were there," she turned to Eriko, who was watching the whole explanation unfold, fascinated.

"Didn't you hear us talking, Eriko-san? When you were clearing up after dinner? I heard you moving around out there in the hall myself," Momoko asked.

Eriko looked up at Penelope and Yamashita san with a confused air.

"I'm sorry, Penny-*sensei*… but yes. I did hear them. I told you that."

Momoko smiled condescendingly at Penelope.

"Now what, Penny-*sensei*? Looks like you've been making the whole thing up to me. I told you, we were there, in the house. After dinner, we went to the library… And she's a witness," she said, pointing at Eriko.

Penelope looked straight back into Momoko's eyes.

"I see," she said and turned to face Eriko.

"Eriko-san, did you *see* Issei or Momoko san after dinner?"

Eriko shook her head.

"No," she said. "I just heard them talking. I told you. About Issei's problem…."

Momoko looked coldly at Eriko.

"His problem? What problem?" she asked. "This is why I got rid of you, Eriko-san. You were always spying on us. And stealing money…."

Eriko sat up indignantly.

"I never took any money from you! And I never spied on you. It's not my fault if I heard you are having a conversation with your brother. Anyone could have heard you!" she shouted at Momoko.

Penny raised her hand and gestured to Eriko to be silent. "Eriko. Tell us what you heard. About Issei's problem…."

Momoko snorted derisively.

"Sure," said Eriko. "I heard him say that he had got someone pregnant and that the girl was hysterical...."

"Did he use the words 'pregnant' and 'hysterical?'" asked Penny mildly.

Eriko paused. "Yes. He did. I heard him say them," she said.

Penny turned to look at Momoko.

"How long did you speak to your brother after dinner, Momoko-san?"

Momoko looked at her strangely. "At least an hour. But we were not talking about any such thing. Issei never said anything about getting anyone pregnant. And that would have been pretty weird if he did, as he didn't like girls. At all. But you probably know that, right?"

Penelope nodded. "Actually, yes, I do," she said. "And I agree; I don't think Issei *did* say that exactly. Would you like me to tell you *exactly* what he said?"

Momoko laughed. "Go on. What *did* he say? I'm dying to know."

"OK, I will," said Penny. "You know, I was at Hokokuji the other day, and all these tourists were passing by, listening to a recording about the place while they walked around. I think quite a lot of places have these things today... Anyway, it got me thinking... and, you know, I think an hour is a long time to talk to someone, particularly if you were trying to stage an alibi. I mean, what are you going to talk about? And you want to make sure your voices would be heard whenever Eriko happened to be passing by. So you needed to be constantly talking. For like, an hour... and I think, to do that, it would be much better if you had *a script*...."

Penelope paused again, and this time Momoko looked at her like she had seen a ghost.

"So, tell me Momoko san. Are you familiar with the play *Whose Afraid of Virginia Woolf?*

Momoko looked down at the floor again, and her hands trembled.

"No… Yes. Maybe, we have a copy. Yes, it was one of my Mama's. She studied drama."

Penny nodded.

"Yes, she did. And you do have a copy of the play, because I saw it. It's there on your bookcase in the library. Eriko saw it too when she was cleaning, and she actually had the book *in her hand* when you saw her with it and fired her… on the spot," she said.

Eriko stared at Momoko, who looked away.

"Anyway, shall we listen to what Issei *actually* said that night?" asked Penelope.

Not waiting for a reply, she reached over to her computer, and an old black and white video appeared on the screen.

"This, Momoko-san, is a recording of the play, and this part, in particular, should be familiar to you. Maybe to Eriko too…."

She turned on the video, and the room filled with the voices of two men.

"I married her because she was pregnant…It was a hysterical pregnancy. She blew up, and then she went down.

"And when she was up, you married her."

"And then she went down."

Penelope stopped the video.

"Shall we play it again? Yes, let's do that…."

She rewound the video and played it a second time.

"I married her because she was pregnant...It was a hysterical pregnancy. She blew up, and then she went down."

Penelope looked at Eriko. "Does that sound familiar, Eriko san?"

Eriko nodded. "Yes... but there was a woman. Not two men...."

"In the play, this discussion does take place between two men... but someone had to play the part of a man in what you heard..." she explained.

Penelope turned to Momoko. "Does it sound familiar to you too, Momoko-san? Of course, it's not something a gay man would ever say to his sister, is it? But it *is* the passage you recorded with Issei in private, and then you left that recording playing in the library for Eriko to hear while you and Issei were in this tea house. And of course, you had told Eriko that you didn't need anything and would call her if you did... So she wasn't going to open the door, was she?"

"And this whole play," Penelope said, gesturing at the screen, "...is just a long dialogue, just people talking in someone's house. And it sounds *just like a conversation*...doesn't it? Which is why you chose it, of course."

Momoko shook her head.

"I don't know what you are talking about," she said, her voice shaking.

Penelope paused for a moment.

"Then I'm sure you won't mind if we have a look at your phone, then? Because there won't be a recording of you and Issei on it, will there? Say... in the 'voice memo' section?" she asked.

214

Momoko looked around at the faces staring at her like a cornered animal.

Penelope closed her laptop and folded her hands.

"There is more to this story, though, and this is something that no one can prove, I'm sorry to say…. and believe me, I wish I could," said Penelope sadly.

"I wonder if you are proud of it… you know, in a way, it *is* the perfect murder. So, we have to say 'bravo' to you in this case. You know what I mean, of course… the marvelous way… you killed your brother," she said matter-of-factly.

Momoko looked at her with hatred in her eyes.

"I never…" she began, but Penelope held up her hand, and she fell silent.

"Hush now, dear. I'll tell the story, just so everyone else here knows. But maybe you can help…."

She turned to Yamashita and the others and then back to Momoko.

"Issei betrayed you, didn't he?" she asked.

Momoko hung her head, and her face disappeared behind the black veil of her hair.

"He changed his mind, the little fiend. Right after Haruko told him about all the lovely money he was going to get as a result of selling the school…."

"Of course, Issei never wanted this life. He never wanted to be an *iemoto*. He never really gave a toss about any of it. He just wanted to be free of the whole thing, really. And when he saw that with his father out of the way, he was going to get, well, everything… It didn't take him long to see that there was much more benefit for *him* in actually

215

going through with the sale *minus* his dear Papa than with him."

"And so, he did the one thing you could not tolerate, didn't he? He agreed to sell… just like his father had. And the result? Well, of course… He had to die as well. It was the only way, wasn't it," she said, staring at Momoko.

Momoko's shoulders began to shake, and it looked like she was sobbing.

"So… you invited him down to this tea house again, and maybe you told him that he really *had* to come and see Dr. Chen and that it would help allay any suspicions she had. You know, as she was the one who had a connection with the police… Just pop in, and stay for a while. Turn on the charm… and, *of course*, you told him that the sweets were safe, that you had checked them yourself… Not to worry."

"And then you watched him… commit suicide…."

There was silence in the room for some time, and Momoko sat trembling on her cushion without saying a word.

"My God…" Haruko breathed, her whispered voice loud in the quiet room.

There was silence for a long moment, and then Penelope leaned over and touched Momoko lightly on the knee. It was a friendly gesture, and unexpected, like waking someone up who had been dreaming.

"The bowl… I should like to see that now. If you could, Momoko san…."

Momoko raised her tear-stained face.

"I know it's here," Penelope said softly. "You wanted it close to you. It's never been to the bank, has it?"

Momoko shook her head and, stretching out her hand, pointed to an old wooden box sitting in the alcove next to the flower arrangement.

"I see. Do you mind if I open it?" she asked.

Getting no reply, Penelope stood and carefully retrieved the box. She then sat back on her cushion again and undid the little green ribband tied around it in the traditional way. With infinite care, she slowly took a small object from inside that had been carefully wrapped in a dark-blue silk cloth and placed it on the floor in the center of the room.

She gently unfolded the cloth, and they all looked at what had been uncovered.

It was an old black ceramic bowl, rough at the edges where you drank and uneven in its proportions, in a way that mirrored the classic Buddhist concept of imperfection.

They all stared at it for a long time.

"It's beautiful," said Yamashita, bowing down to get a closer look. "It's just what I imagined something of his would look like....."

Penelope nodded. "If I were you, I wouldn't drink from it. Not until it's been properly cleaned...."

Chapter 20

The House Among The Roses

Two weeks later...

Though the invitations were rare, there was nothing Penelope and Fei enjoyed more than a meal at the Chief Inspector's home.

Yamashita lived in an old house just off the little road leading to the famous Meigetsu-in temple in Kita-Kamakura, which was hard by the much larger Engakuji temple where his brother Dokan served.

It was a large two-story Western-style house that their parents had bought and renovated when they had retired, but with its wonderfully atmospheric location and its proximity to the town these days, it was a much sought-after home. It had dark, highly polished cedar floors and, unusually for a house of its age, not a single tatami mat room. It had a spacious kitchen and living room, and best of all, there was a large glass conservatory that opened out onto a magnificent lawned garden. This garden, which had been planted largely by the inspector's late mother, was filled with roses of every description, these having been her favorites, and also maple and cherry trees, which had been his father's joy to see in their seasons.

On these rare occasions when the inspector did open his house to his friends, usually around the time the roses or the hydrangea were in bloom, or occasionally in the autumn such as today, his brother would often join them for dinner. The kitchen on these occasions would be mainly turned over to Penelope and Dokan, as the Inspector was perfectly content to confine himself to choosing the wine and leave them to it. His brother, being a Buddhist monk, never touched meat or alcohol, so there was always a selection of vegetarian dishes on the menu, of which fortunately Dokan was a master.

That evening the maples in the garden were in their full glory, a drifting cloud of red and gold falling across the green of the manicured lawns in the dying light of the late afternoon.

Penelope was in the kitchen with Dokan, watching the monk washing and slicing the vegetables, whereas Fei and Yamashita were in the conservatory attacking the first bottle of wine.

For Penelope, something about the way Dokan did these simple tasks spoke of his years of Zen training. Many monks had to spend their early years in the monastery kitchen, where they learned how to cook for everybody else and also worked in the gardens where the food was grown. Dokan himself had been no exception, and he always said that the kitchen was the best place in the monastery to learn about Zen.

Watching him work, Penelope observed that there did not seem to be a wasted motion nor any waste of food. He poured the water into a container rather than simply washing the vegetables under the tap, and when he had finished carefully washing each individual item, he took the water outside and poured it at the base of several plants. Even the vegetable scraps he carefully kept for the compost, and whenever he cut or peeled something, there was a slowness and precision to the way his knife moved that bespoke a formidable attention, as compared to Penelope or Fei, who chopped things up as quickly as possible while they were speaking and were barely aware of what they were doing from one moment to the next.

Although neither of them commented on the way the other cooked, Penelope always thought of working in the kitchen with Dokan as like being in the meditation hall with him. When she was alone at home after being with him, she often thought of the need to slow down and be more aware of what she was doing. She found that cultivating this attitude as she worked gave her the same peace of mind that she enjoyed in her weekly visits to Engakuji.

With the meal finally prepared, they joined the others in the conservatory, where they were enjoying a glass of wine and discussing *shogi*, which they planned to play after dinner.

"My brother tells me you have continued to be very useful to him lately, Penny-*sensei*?" said Dokan with a smile as they sat down. "Does this mean you are going to turn into a police officer too? I seem to be surrounded by them. It's like I'm about to be arrested."

The monk was dressed tonight in a simple dark blue tunic and matching trousers of the kind that monks and many other Japanese manual workers wear when they are outside

220

on the job, rather than in his usual robes. Penelope always liked these traditional working clothes, and she had a similar set that she sometimes wore at home or in the garden herself.

Looking at him tonight, there was something about the simple and uncomplicated elegance of his appearance that Penelope liked, a lack of pretence that spoke to his sense of the equality that existed between them.

Fei was having none of his comment, however.

"Hey, I'm not police," she said, "I just work there."

"And get paid by them," chided Yamashita.

"That's not the same thing. Just because you work in the zoo doesn't make you a panda," remonstrated Fei with a smile.

Dokan laughed. "You didn't answer my question, Penny-*sensei*. You're not thinking of changing professions, are you?"

Penelope shook her head. "Not a chance. Not at my age."

Yamashita poured her some wine.

"I rather hoped you would. I'd hire you in a shot," said the inspector. "You should see the way she interrogates a suspect. I wish I had a video of it to show the younger detectives I have to work with... they could learn something."

Penny smiled and waved away the compliment.

"I should leave that to the experts in future," she replied modestly.

Yamashita shook his head.

"Absolutely not. You completely destroyed her. I couldn't have done it better myself, and I have thirty years of experience interviewing suspects," he said admiringly.

"I'm curious about a couple of things however, if you don't mind me bringing up work on such a nice evening…" he said, looking around the room as if to ask for permission.

Dokan shook his head.

"My brother has never been capable of leaving work at the office. He is like a dog with a bone. Always takes it with him."

"Now, you can't talk," he said, wagging a finger at the monk. "Anyway, my question, Penny-*sensei*, is what made you first suspect it was Momoko? I thought you liked her. Most people don't suspect the people they like of double murder."

"Except for policemen," interjected Dokan.

Yamashita smiled.

"Maybe true…" he said.

Penelope looked out the conservatory's glass windows and saw the last rays of sunlight slowly disappear from the lawn. As the hills behind Kamakura lay to the west, the sunset always seemed to come more suddenly here.

"Well, I can tell you the answer, but Fei is probably going to get mad with me," she smiled.

Fei looked up at her.

"Not the…" she began.

Penelope held up her hand for silence and finished her sentence.

"Yes. The light. It was the first thing I noticed. The light was off. And that got me thinking, of course, as no one commits suicide in the dark. So someone turned it off. Simple as that. Momoko was too smart to do that, and she simply didn't notice that Issei had turned it off. Maybe she went up to the house first. It would have been easier to slip back in that way if it was just one person. And poor Issei, with his OCD, probably didn't even notice what he was doing. He just waited a minute, switched off the light, and followed her up to the house. And Haruko was out, we know that… so…" she looked up at Yamashita.

"Momoko," he said simply.

"Yes… well, someone anyhow. But it wasn't a suicide. It was planned. And Issei was no planner," said Penelope quietly.

Yamashita nodded.

"That was very observant of you," he said.

Penelope shrugged.

"Something she no doubt learned in my meditation class," said Dokan cheerfully.

"No doubt," said the inspector wryly. "But also there was the note… that was very clever actually. We never thought of that when we dusted the keyboard…."

"The note? I never heard that story," said Fei. "Does anyone want more wine? I do…"

Yamashita poured her another glass.

"It was a suggestion Penny-*sensei* made afterward," he said. "After we arrested Momoko-san. She suggested we look at the keyboard. It was just a small thing, and of course, we found Momoko's prints on the keyboard, but there was nothing really incriminating in that, she could have just been using her father's computer for some reason…."

Penelope nodded.

"Except Momoko had her own laptop and phone, and she even had her own printer in her bedroom. So why would she use Papa's? Except for…" she said.

"Writing the note," finished Fei. "But as you said, she could have just been using his computer for some other mundane reason, like maybe her's wasn't working for some reason."

The inspector wagged his finger at her.

"That's true. Except we know it was Momoko who wrote that note on that computer."

"How?" asked Dokan.

The inspector smiled.

"Because Penny-*sensei* here told us we should compare the letters of the note with the keys we found Momoko's prints on. It was a very short note, and we found her prints only on the exact letters used in the note. Not on any of the other alphabet keys…."

"Wow…" said Dokan, impressed. "Well done, Penny-*sensei*."

Penelope looked at the floor.

"It's not enough to hang someone on," said the inspector, "But added to the rest of the evidence, it certainly doesn't hurt."

"That's true…" said Fei. "So, did Momoko confess to it all?"

Yamashita took off his glasses and cleaned them with a small towel.

"Not at all. She hasn't said a word. That girl's a lot stronger than she looks. Although I think thanks to Penny-*sensei* here we have her dead to rights on her father's murder… but… all the same."

"But what about Issei?" asked his brother.

"Issei… yes…well," he sighed.

224

Penelope looked up, "Issei… that was always going to be impossible to prove. Did she tell him to come? Did she say the sweets were fine?"

She took a swig of her wine and shrugged. "That, friends, we may never know. Like I said to her, it's the perfect murder," she said reflectively.

There was silence among them for a moment.

"Do you believe in that?" Dokan asked his brother quietly.

The inspector eyed him carefully, then shook his head.

"The perfect murder? No. I don't. I just believe there are some murders where we cannot prove who did it. For the moment. But perfect… no. There is always some mistake. There is always some chance that new evidence will come to light. Or maybe even that the murderer will one day change their minds and confess. It happens…"

Penelope nodded. "Yes, it does. Taking a life is a messy thing. There are always a lot of moving parts. Eventually, someone may put them together, and voila, you have your proof. Until then, all you have left are the pieces of the jigsaw."

"What about that play? How did you know it was *that* play?" she asked, "and how did you know she had not deleted the recording from her phone?"

"I didn't. I was bluffing. And the play? That… was just blind good luck. I just noticed that it was the only play not put back in its place on the shelf that day. Like someone had been using it… and then I was in the library… and I just happened to see the drama section and…."

"You followed up on a loose end. That's exactly what a good cop would do," said Yamashita with a smile. "I can't tell you how many villains get away with it because loose ends are not followed up. Details. That's where you find the devil, as my old boss used to say...."

"So what's going to happen to her? Is she going to swing?" asked Fei.

"Oh, Fei..." reproved Penelope. "Really..."

"I'm just stating the obvious. It's just a question..." said Fei.

"Well, the answer to that question is probably not," said Yamashita. "We can't prove Issei's murder. We can only infer it. So it's really up to the jury. We're going to charge her with it for sure, but we'll just have to wait and see. And even if they sentence her to death, you know what it's like here, she could sit on death row for twenty years and still get off on appeal."

"True," said Fei.

Yamashita stood up and motioned them into the dining room, where they took their seats, and Penelope and Dokan busied themselves with serving the food.

"I think the biggest problem, actually... the biggest problem with this case from the beginning," said Yamashita, "has been motive... Motive is always key. And when you are a cop, the motive is usually about the question of who benefits. That's the thing you always look at."

"I presume you are talking about money now? You know, I do miss these conversations around the table in the monastery," said Dokan with a slight roll of his eyes as he placed his chopsticks neatly on the chopstick rest next to his plate.

Everybody smiled, and his brother shrugged helplessly.

"Well, you know... police... But it's true. If you look at motive, which, you're right, is usually money, it's venal, I know, but… if you look at who benefits financially, the answer is whoever inherits after they sell the school and the Rikyu bowl and clear the debts. With the father out of the way, it's unclear, however. The debts were substantial, so there was absolutely no financial benefit in killing him if you were not going to sell. That puts Momoko in the clear, at least as far as that motive goes, as she would be killing people so she can inherit a bankrupt tea school. And that makes no sense, of course. Believe me, her lawyer will be making that argument, of that I'm sure," he said.

Penelope agreed.

"That was the confusing issue with this. But as you know, especially with women, it's not always about the money…" she said.

"It is as far as I'm concerned," Fei laughed. "I just want the cash. It's lucky my relatives don't have any. For them…"

"I see," said Dokan. "Remind me to mention that to your aunt next time. So how did you work out why she did this, Penny-*sensei*? Was it female intuition? That's another thing we tend to lack where I live…."

Penelope smiled.

"Well, actually, I don't have much intuition either. Not any that I would trust, at least," she said. "The fact is, I got help from a nice old gentleman who bought me a coffee and explained all about Kamakura history."

She helped herself to a plate of beans and tofu.

"And who pray was that?" asked Fei.

Penelope paused a moment.

"It's strange the people you meet, some of them, the ones you least expect, are the ones who help you the most."

She looked at Dokan, who was busying himself with his meal and did not look up.

"Anyway, this gentleman used to be a teacher, and then he retired and took up history, and he also wrote a small book on the tea ceremony. And he knew about the Takahashi's. When he told me that Momoko and Issei were direct descendants of Sen no Rikyu, it all fell into place for me. Now that couldn't possibly be a motive for Issei and Haruko, they couldn't care less about history and wanted to sell the place lock, stock and barrel. But Momoko... she was different. She is a history major with a great attachment to the tea ceremony and her mother's memory... That's why she kept all her books.... She cared. She really cared. And that... that's motive, I think."

Yamashita nodded.

"It is," he agreed.

Dokan sighed and put down his chopsticks again.

"So, she killed her family over tea bowls," he said with a sigh.

"Nice," Fei grinned, "that about sums it up."

"It does, I'm afraid..." the monk said, "And the strange thing is, if you know the history, that this 'daughter of Rikyu' committed these terrible crimes in the name of continuing his legacy. The legacy of the tea ceremony. Whereas Rikyu himself would have been appalled at that idea. He always said the tea ceremony should be about simple things and that the aim was to see the beauty of the everyday objects around you. *Wabi,* you know. The color of the tea. The sunlight shining on the tatami floor. The sound the water makes in the kettle...."

He looked around at them.

"Tea bowls? Really? That's so sad, I find..." he said quietly.

Penelope and he exchanged a long look, and then she nodded and smiled.

"It is, isn't it," she said. "But that's life... sometimes, we just get caught up in our own dreams."

About the Author

Ash Warren is an Australian author who graduated with a degree in medieval history and English literature from the University of New South Wales in Sydney.

After a period of roaming the world with a backpack, he settled in Japan where he has now lived since 1992. During that time he has written and published widely on language and Japanese Culture and teaches at a university in Tokyo.

He is the author of *The Way of Salt: Sumo and the Culture of Japan, The Language Code,* and *Mastering the Japanese Writing System.* (Also available at Amazon and elsewhere.)

He lives with his family in Tokyo with one dog, two cats and has a penchant for chess, sumo, classical music, and talking about politics over too much sake.

Dark Tea is the first book in the Penelope Middleton series!

If you would like to be updated about further books in the series, please go to:

www.arwarren.net

And subscribe!

Printed in Great Britain
by Amazon

12378914R00133